QUICK ON THE DRAW

Luke Chance has one claim to fame: he's real quick on the draw. Trying to outrun a reputation he doesn't want, he ends up in Rattlesnake Springs — where he meets the beautiful Teddy Austin. Teddy hires him to break horses on her father's ranch, but pretty soon Luke is locking horns with the Shadow Hills foreman, Thad McClory. As if that wasn't enough, the Austins are also having trouble with their neighbors. Though he doesn't want to get involved, it seems Luke can't help but do so . . .

STEVE HAYES

QUICK ON
THE DRAW

Complete and Unabridged

LINFORD
Leicester

First published in Great Britain in 2016

First Linford Edition
published 2017

A catalogue record for this book is available
from the British Library.

ISBN 978–1–4448–3413–0

Published by
F. A. Thorpe (Publishing)
Anstey, Leicestershire

Set by Words & Graphics Ltd.
Anstey, Leicestershire
Printed and bound in Great Britain by
T.J. International Ltd., Padstow, Cornwall

This book is printed on acid-free paper

For Ethan Thompson

Prologue

Six months ago, while still in the chips, Luke Chance rode through the sun-baked outskirts of El Paso and reined up outside an old mission facing the Mexican border. He hadn't been there in years, but just the sight of the crumbling adobe walls and damaged bell-tower topped by a broken wooden cross brought childhood memories flooding back to him. Dismounting outside the chapel, the rear of which was attached to a now-abandoned orphanage, he tied his sweat-caked buckskin to a bush, hung his gun-belt over the saddle and approached the entrance.

The door was scarred and its strap-hinges so worn, it hung at a forlorn angle as if to remind visitors, and perhaps God, what a sorry condition the mission had fallen into. He was neither a religious nor emotional man. He'd experienced enough of life's suffering and death to not believe in much of anything anymore. But as he paused before the smooth, well-trodden door-step he couldn't help thinking of his ma, Rosalie, a woman he barely remembered, telling him to sit there and wait until she returned. Of course, she —

'Por favor, senor, puedo ayudarle?'

A frail voice asking if she could help him interrupted his memories. He turned and saw a gaunt old nun wearing a traditional black habit and white coif, both of which were well-worn and badly frayed at the edges. A silver cross hung from a black cord around her neck and wooden rosary beads dangled from her clasped hands.

Removing his hat, he said: 'Hablas ingles, sister?'

'Si, senor. Un poquito.'

'Bueno. I'm . . . uh . . . looking for Sister Ines de la Cruz.'

'Ah-h,' the old nun said sadly. 'La hermana Ines, she is . . . uh . . . most sick, senor.'

'So I heard. That's why I came.' He pointed to the crumbling orphanage. 'I grew up here.'

The old nun frowned and Luke sensed she didn't understand.

Groping for the right words, he pointed to himself, said: 'Creci . . . aqui.'

'Oh, si, si . . . ' She gave a crinkly smile, 'You come,' and beckoned for him to follow her. Hat in hand, he entered the chapel behind her. It was cool and dim inside. Overhead the wind moaned in the empty bell-tower. Then, as if out of respect, it hushed. Now the only sound was the muffled tap-tapping of their footsteps as the two of them walked down the aisle toward a rear door.

Around him the white-washed walls were stained yellow by rain that had leaked in through the damaged roof. Poles of sunlight shined through cracks in the walls, their brightness illuminating the rows of old broken pews. A veil of dust covered everything except the altar and the life-like crucifix on the wall behind it. Both were spotless, as if polished by hand,

and as Luke walked past them he could have sworn he heard the pure-toned, high-pitched tenor voices of the choir-boys singing an alabado.

One of the voices was his. It seemed so real he could barely believe he was imagining it. Hell, he could even remember the words of the hymn. Unnerved, he forced himself to forget the past and followed the old nun through the door and along a dim, narrow corridor that led to the infirmary. When they reached the entryway, she motioned for him to wait and disappeared inside.

While waiting, he felt strangely intimidated by his surroundings, as if he were a child again, and instantly regretted coming. It wasn't too late to leave, he told himself. But before he could, the old nun reappeared and motioned for him to enter. He did. This time she didn't accompany him and he walked alone between the rows of rusted iron cots, none of which had mattresses, until he came to the end bed. Here, wrapped in a blanket, lay a small, frail woman whose face was so shriveled and pale he didn't recognize her. Wisps of gray hair poked from under the white wimple covering her head, her sunken eyes were closed and she was barely breathing.

Not wanting to believe that this was Sister Ines de la Cruz, the nun who had had such an impact on his life, Luke was about to leave when she opened her eyes.

They flickered momentarily, as if trying to focus, and then as they saw him life seemed to enter them, turning them from dull brown to sparkling amber.

He knew those eyes. They had watched him grow up, sometimes scolding, sometimes happy, but always caring.

He smiled.

He wanted her to smile back, so that he knew she'd recognized him, but she didn't. Instead, all life left her eyes, returning them to dull brown, and by her blank stare he knew he'd lost her for good.

Luke leaned down and kissed her cold forehead. It was like kissing a statue. Feeling empty inside, he left the infirmary by a rear door and walked out into the hot glaring sunlight.

There was no sign of the old nun and the chapel door was closed. Needing a drink, he mounted up and rode on into town. The intense heat had driven most of the townspeople indoors, leaving the streets almost empty. He finally reached East San Antonio Avenue and reined in the buckskin outside the Acme Saloon. An old wood-and-adobe building, it had a reputation for unwatered whiskey and honest dealers who never dealt from the bottom of the deck. It was also frequented by a surly, mean-tempered gunman named John Wesley Hardin, a killer Luke had no respect for, and he hoped he wouldn't run into him, guessing it might end up with them shooting it out.

Dismounting, Luke wrapped the reins around the hitch-rail. He was relieved to see there were only two other horses tied up beside the buckskin. This meant the saloon wasn't crowded, which lessened the odds that he'd be recognized from the wanted posters pinned up in

6

the marshal's office.

Entering, he stood by the door until his eyes got accustomed to the dimness and then made his way past the poker tables to the bar in back. The players didn't even look up as he passed and the three old-timers drinking at the bar merely glanced his way then returned to their conversation.

Poker was Luke's nemesis. He loved the game and considered himself a skillful player, but lately bad luck had dogged him and he usually wound up with empty pockets. But not today — he resisted the urge to sit in on one of the games and went to the end of the bar. From here he could watch the door in case any lawmen entered, and either get the drop on them or escape out the back door.

The bartender approached and Luke ordered a beer. A big fleshy man with a large waxed mustache and a gleaming bald dome, he only looked at Luke for a moment but something in his eyes warned the outlaw that the bartender had recognized him and wasn't happy to see him.

'Drink up,' he told Luke when he returned with the beer, 'and then make some dust.'

Luke ignored him. He'd traveled far in the past few days and was in no mood to be rushed. Blowing the froth from his beer, he took a long gulp. Nothing ever tasted better. Luke drained the glass with a second gulp, put a nickel on the bar and signaled to the bartender to pour him another.

He came up empty-handed, square-eyed Luke, and placing both hands under the bar, said: 'Your money's no good here, mister.'

'Then pour me a free one.'

The bartender's lips tightened and he started to bring something out from under the bar.

'Don't,' Luke warned. 'A beer ain't worth dying for.'

The bartender froze.

''Sides,' Luke added softly, 'two's my limit.'

The bartender licked the underside of his mustache and tried to stare Luke down. When he couldn't, he decided not to prod him. Luke watched him walk to the tap, pull the handle down and fill the glass. He then returned and set the beer on the bar.

'Look, mister,' he said as Luke enjoyed his beer, 'I don't got nothing against you personally. But this town's full of young guns all itching to make a name for themselves, and killing the fastest gun around would make them heroes. So the longer you stay here, the more likelihood there is of word spreading and — ' He broke off as Luke set his empty glass down.

'Got a wet towel handy?'

The bartender grabbed one from beneath the bar and gave it to Luke, who wiped his face with it and then around his neck inside his shirt collar. Refreshed and feeling like a new man. Luke dropped the towel on the bar and walked out.

Outside, a tall skinny youth armed

with two six-guns in low-slung, tied-down holsters was examining the buckskin. Having a stranger standing so close made the horse nervous and it snorted and shied away.

'Son,' Luke said quietly, 'you looking to buy or just nosing around?'

The youth froze and then slowly turned to face Luke. He had a thin, almost chinless face that was hard to like, made all the more unpleasant by pimples.

'Neither,' he said, hands dropping to his fancy bone-handled Colts. 'I'm here to prove you ain't the fastest gun alive.'

'You don't have to prove nothing,' Luke said amiably. 'If building your reputation's what you're after, I'm more than happy to admit you can jerk your iron faster than me. Hell, I'll even drink to it.'

The pimply youth smirked. 'I ain't interested in bending elbows with you, mister. I just want to collect that reward on your head.'

Luke sensed the youth meant what

he said and knew it wasn't going to be easy to make him back down. Luke also sensed the youth's confidence was based on something more than his fast draw and without moving his head, eyed both sides of the street, looking for someone who might be backing his play. He didn't see anyone at first. But then he glimpsed a rifle barrel poking out of an alley across the street.

'Some other time,' Luke said pleasantly. 'When it ain't so damned hot, maybe.'

His tone misled the youth and he got cocky. 'Save your breath,' he sneered. 'I aim to kill you whether you slap leather or not.'

Luke knew then he had to shoot the youth and it made him deep-down angry.

'Don't be a damned fool,' he snarled. 'You so much as twitch and I'll kill you — you and your gutless pal across the street.'

Luke hoped his threat would scare the youth off. But it didn't. He grabbed for his guns.

Luke drew and fired before the youth's weapons had cleared leather. Then as he crumpled — eyes wide with shock and a hole in his heart — Luke shot his friend as he stepped out of the alley, rifle already pressed against his shoulder.

The two shots sounded like one. Both youths fell on their faces and didn't move.

Luke holstered his Colt almost as quickly as he'd drawn it.

The townspeople watching from the boardwalks gaped, unable to believe anyone could draw that fast.

Unfazed, Luke waited a moment to see if there was anyone else gunning for him. There wasn't. He untied the buckskin, mounted and rode off.

Before he reached the corner he passed the marshal's office. The tall, gray-haired lawman stood in the door-way calmly lighting a long black cigar. He'd recognized Luke and knew better than to brace him. Exhaling a stream of smoke, he tipped the brim of his tan, high-crowned *Stetson* in acknowledgement.

Luke nodded back to him, smiling to himself as he saw a strait-laced, middle-aged busybody confront the lawman. Though unable to hear their conversation Luke knew the woman was demanding what every other citizen in every other town demanded — why the devil wasn't the marshal arresting this known outlaw. Unruffled, the lawman took out his fob watch, indicated the time and then pointed to *Polly's Café* across the street. Right now, Luke thought, amused, he's explaining that the cook is grilling a steak for him and he can't disappoint her.

On reaching the corner, Luke looked back at the marshal. He was crossing the street, contentedly puffing on his cigar and seemed at peace with the world.

Luke envied him. And as he rode on, he wondered if he'd ever be as happy.

Somehow he doubted it.

1

They kicked him off the stagecoach at Rattlesnake Springs.

It riled Luke, but he didn't blame them. Both the driver and the shotgun guard were stand-up *hombres* and he knew if it had been up to them, they would have let him ride to the end of the line at Santa Rosa, a small but fast-growing town in southwest New Mexico. But as the driver had explained when they picked Luke up on the trail, it wasn't up to him or the guard. There were passengers to consider. If they found out that he or the guard had broken the rules and given Luke a free ride, they might report them which could possibly cost them their jobs.

So Luke didn't grumble or cause a fuss but spent his last dollar on a ticket to Rattlesnake Springs, the second of three swing stations servicing the local stage-line that carried passengers and the U.S. mail between El Paso and Santa Rosa.

There was no room in the coach, so, Winchester in hand, he climbed on top and sat with his back to the baggage roped down behind him. Under the blazing hot sun it was like sitting in a furnace. He was already tired from an all-night poker game, which unsurprisingly had left him broke, so he pulled his old flat-crowned Stetson over his eyes and with the wind-blown sand stinging his face and the coach jolting under him like an untamed bronc, tried to get some sleep. It wasn't easy but he was so damned beat, he finally dozed off.

Two hours later, as the stage approached the tiny settlement, someone yelling startled him awake. It was the shotgun guard. He was leaning down over the side of the coach shouting to the passengers that they were only stopping long enough to change teams, so if anyone needed water or to relieve themselves, they better do it fast as the stage was already behind schedule and wouldn't wait for anyone.

Thanks to his warning, Luke wasn't surprised when they reined up before the collection of shacks and log cabins to see a handler already waiting with fresh horses. He jumped down from the coach, leaned his rifle against a rear wheel and started unhitching the weary team. It wasn't his job, but he felt obliged to the driver for slipping him a quarter earlier so he could buy some grub and knew that the faster the teams were changed the better chance the stage had to get back on schedule.

A few minutes later the driver threw Luke a grateful wave then cracked his whip over the horses and the stage pulled out of the settlement and raced on toward Santa Rosa.

Wishing he was still on board, Luke watched the coach leave amid swirling dust and then looked about him. Beyond the settlement, as far as he could see,

17

the desert scrubland stretched to the horizon. Heat waves reflected off the sunbaked sand, the glare making him squint. It was a harsh desolate country, dry as parched lips and plagued by sidewinders, Gila monsters, jack rabbits and gaunt coyotes that ate everything from beetles to carrion. But they weren't the only creatures fighting to survive in this desert hellhole. Now and then Mexican wolves wandered up from the nearby border, while red-tail hawks hovered above the distant brown foothills, wings outstretched, balancing on the thermals as they too looked for prey among the cacti and snake grass fringing the dry riverbeds.

He felt his stomach rumble. It reminded Luke just how hungry he was and rifle in hand, he hurried to the shack that served chow.

2

Hot as it was outside, it was even hotter in the grub shack. There was no window and because of the swirling, wind-blown sand the door had to be kept closed, trapping the intense heat. Worse, everything smelled of burned grease. As if the stench wasn't enough to contend with, all the cooking was done on an old wood-burning stove in one corner. It belched smoke and Luke had barely gotten seated at the table when his already-raw eyes began to sting.

He rubbed his eyes but that only made them worse. He was blinking like a bat at sunup when a sweaty, fat-faced woman with blubbery chins and straggly red hair came wheezing out of the kitchen. According to the driver she was called Momma Cake, though he didn't know why since she only baked pies. Luke had seen lots of fat women in his travels, but none as fat as her. She looked enormous in a purple dress that was spattered with grease and food stains. It was at least two sizes too small for her, and squeezing herself into it had caused the top button to pop off and the seams under her bulging arms to burst open.

Now most girls Luke knew thought he looked good enough to take to bed. But Momma Cake wasn't one of them. She shot him a look that would have soured milk and in a gravelly voice, said: 'If you want more than coffee, cowboy, I'll see your money first.'

He dug out his quarter and put it on the table. 'What'll that buy me?'

'Steak and eggs, for starters.'

'How about 'taters?'

'Included.'

'Coffee?'

'Same.'

'Then fire up the stove, ma'am.'

He expected her to smile. But her sour expression never changed as she yelled to someone in the kitchen. 'Girl, where's that damn' water I told you to fetch?'

Moments later a scrawny young Navaho girl, dressed in doeskin and with braids reaching to her shoulders, timidly squeezed past Momma Cake and set a kettle of water atop the stove.

'Next time I have to repeat myself,' Momma Cake warned, 'you'll wish I'd sold you to the Comanches! Now, move your bony ass and get me some kindling.'

The girl didn't say anything. Keeping her head down, as if trying to hide something, she hurried past Luke. Curious, he turned and watched her. Her back was to him but as she opened the door and went out, he caught a glimpse of her face and saw she had a black eye.

'What happened to her?' he asked as Momma Cake approached the table.

'How the hell should I know?' she said. 'Lazy, good-for-nothing little . . . she's always running into something.'

'Like your fist, maybe?'

Momma Cake ignored his insinuation. She shot him another sour look, picked up his quarter and bit it with her broken front teeth. Satisfied that it wasn't a dud, she dropped it in her pocket and went to the stove. Stirring the embers, she closed the stove door and dropped a slab of gristly meat into a frying pan full of sizzling grease. She added hash browns and while they were cooking, filled a chipped porcelain mug with oily black coffee.

'You got a nickel in change coming,' she said as she brought his food to the table. 'Either that or a slice of berry pie. Which'll it be?'

'I'll take the pie,' Luke said.

Momma Cake waddled to a counter. There, she scooped a wedge of berry pie from a dish, set it on the table before him and re-entered the kitchen. He couldn't see what she was doing but it sounded like she was gathering up pots and pans.

He cut into the fatty meat and began eating. It was tough chewing but he was so hungry he didn't care. He wolfed the steak down, took a gulp of coffee and started on his pie.

As he did, he heard horsemen approaching. The loud din coming from the kitchen hid how many riders there were, but Luke counted at least six or seven. Unlike Texas, he wasn't wanted for anything in New Mexico, but he still instinctively reached for his six-gun. It wasn't in his holster. He glanced down, momentarily surprised, and then remembered pawning his Colt Peacemaker and saddle in El Paso for gambling money. Cursing his sorry state of affairs and his bad luck at the poker tables, he grabbed his rifle and leaned it against the table, within easy reach, and went on eating.

Just then the cabin door opened. Luke turned around, expecting to see the Navaho girl returning with the kindling.

That was when he saw her. She wasn't the most beautiful girl he'd ever seen. Hell, he'd known dancing girls who were prettier and a few saloon whores who had sexier figures, but the truth was none of them affected him like she did.

Just by walking past him to the kitchen she made his heart pound.

She wasn't tall, but because of the erect way she carried herself she looked tall. She had strong features, pouty lips that made her look sultry and long autumn-colored hair pulled back in a bun. He guessed she was his age or a tad younger, yet exuded a maturity beyond her years. There was also something dangerous about her. Luke couldn't pinpoint what it was, but that didn't scare him off. Truth is it made her all the more appealing and he couldn't take his eyes off her.

He watched her as she stood confidently in the kitchen doorway, impatiently slapping her riding gloves against her hip while waiting for Momma Cake to join her.

Finally, the clattering of pots and pans stopped and Momma Cake appeared, her fat sweaty face all smiles.

'Hiyah, Miss Teddy,' she gushed. 'Lordy, this is a pleasant surprise.'

'Not for me,' grumbled the girl. 'Our

wrangler — ' She broke off as a bulky dark-haired man in his fifties entered and joined her. Luke didn't hear everything they said, but caught enough to know the man was her foreman.

When they had finished talking, the girl named Teddy turned back to Momma Cake. 'As I was saying, our wrangler, Zach Grady, was thrown from his horse as we were crossing Gila Flats. I hated to shoot her — she was the best mare in our *remuda* — but she'd gone lame so I had no choice. Under normal circumstances I would have had Zach ride double. But his leg's badly broken and besides, in this awful heat I was worried that his extra weight might break down another horse — '

'You want to borrow my wagon, that it?' Momma Cake interrupted.

'Yes. Naturally I'll pay you — '

'That ain't necessary. Your pa's always treated me square.'

'Nevertheless, I still want to pay. What's more, I'll make sure one of the boys brings the wagon back to you first thing tomorrow morning. Fair enough?'

Momma Cake nodded fatly. 'I'll tell my handler to hitch up the team.'

'Thanks.' Teddy turned to her foreman. 'Thad, have the men help Zach into the wagon. I'll be right out.'

He nodded, sized Luke up for a moment, seemed satisfied he posed no threat and walked out.

3

Luke had eaten his meal and was finishing his coffee when Teddy approached him, asking: 'By any chance, cowboy, are you looking for work?'

Hoping his luck had just changed, but not wanting to seem over-eager, he said cautiously: 'Maybe. Why?'

'Well, as you may have just heard, one of my men broke his leg and — '

'What kind of work?'

'Well, Grady was top wrangler, but I don't expect you to take his place. I'd be happy if you could help out till the roundup is over. I'll pay fair wages.'

'What if I *could* take his place? What kind of wages would you pay then?'

'That would depend on how good you are at breaking wild mustangs.'

'The best.'

She eyed Luke skeptically, eyes gray

as a wintry sky. 'Sure don't sell yourself short, do you?'

Luke grinned. 'A fella once said, it ain't bragging if you can back it up.'

She hesitated and nibbled her lip, still not fully convinced.

'Tell you what, ma'am. If I can't handle the job or don't live up to your expectations, you don't have to pay me one cent.'

That sold her.

'Fair enough. As for wages, if you're as good as you say, I'll pay top dollar.'

'Then I'm your man — on one condition.'

'Name it.'

'You throw in a saddle and one of the broomtails I break.'

'That's asking a lot.'

'You're getting a lot.'

'I'd better be. Anything else?'

'Nope.'

'Then consider yourself hired. Oh, by the way,' she added, 'I'm Luther Austin's daughter, Teddy.'

'Teddy?'

'Actually it's Theodosia, but I find that a bit of a mouthful, don't you?'

Luke did something with his shoulders that could have meant anything.

'Ah,' she said, 'one of those.'

'One of what?'

'A proponent of the noncommittal.'

'Say again?'

'You know? Folks who shrug rather than give their opinion.'

'Maybe I don't have an opinion.'

'That's even worse.'

'Reckon I'm damned either way, then.'

'One step closer to purgatory.'

He sensed she was needling him, but wasn't sure how far he could prod her.

She studied him for another moment then smiled. 'You didn't.'

'Didn't what?'

'Make a mistake by agreeing to work for me. That's what you were thinking, wasn't it?'

It was, but he sure as hell wasn't going to admit it.

'Relax, cowboy. I'm just funning with you.'

'How's that going to work when you're my boss?'

'That's something you'll never have to worry about. Once we get to the ranch, I'll be so busy you won't know I'm around, Mister — uh?'

'Luke . . . Luke Chance . . . but most everyone calls me L.C.'

'Then that's what I'll call you,' she said. 'Now, come on outside and I'll introduce you to Thad McClory, my foreman.'

4

Texas and New Mexico were known for big ranches and Luke had drawn wages at most of them. Even so, he was impressed by the size of Shadow Hills. It stretched the entire length of the San Dimas Valley all the way to the outskirts of Santa Rosa.

It took them half a day of hard riding to reach the arched entrance that warned trespassers they were entering private property, and another hour or so to reach the main house. By then, Luke had had more than his fill of sitting in the wagon. He was not only soaked with sweat but like Grady, huddled in pain beside him, felt as if every bone in his body had been jarred loose.

The ranch-house was bigger than some hotels he'd seen. It was three stories high and each story was encircled by a shaded veranda. Every window had a breath-taking view of the valley and the distant brown hills that rose up on all sides like protective walls. But the hills weren't as peaceful and serene as they looked. Though it was the summer of 1888 and local politicians liked to brag about how New Mexico was civilized and safe from marauding Indians, according to Teddy there were Comanches and Comancheros hiding out in the hills and anyone riding through them did so at their own risk.

'Come inside,' she said as Luke jumped down from the wagon. 'I want you to meet my father.'

Luke wasn't anxious to meet him, having heard rumors that described him as bitter and domineering, but knew better than to argue. As they walked to the house and climbed the porch steps, he noticed how McClory and the men were watching him. They looked resentful, as if they felt he was getting special treatment.

He ignored them. Hell, it wasn't his fault that their boss had taken a liking to him. It had just happened, like always. Call it luck of the draw, but for some reason the owners of all the ranches he'd worked at always treated him like he was family. As a result, the other hands became jealous and resented him, just like now, and over the years he'd been forced to live with it.

Removing his hat and holding his rifle at his side, Luke followed Teddy into the house. Inside, everything was equally impressive. The entrance hall alone was big enough to hold a harvest hoedown. They continued on, passing a large red-carpeted staircase leading to the upper floors. Beyond the stairs in a candlelit alcove, stood a marble pedestal on top of which sat the bust of a Confederate cavalry officer. Though he was staring straight ahead his eyes seemed to follow Luke everywhere. Even more unsettling, he seemed to be glaring at him for daring to be with his daughter.

'Come on, L.C.,' Teddy insisted as Luke slowed down. 'Don't be shy. Father won't bite you — even though I'm sure many folks have told you differently.'

'Nobody's told me nothing about your pa,' he lied. 'Good or bad.'

'They haven't?' She looked surprised. 'Well, that's a change.' She led him to the end of the hall, on into a large, high-ceilinged parlor with tapestries and paintings on the walls, fine handcrafted furniture and an enormous fireplace. Made of huge stone, it was shaped like a cathedral window and tall enough for him to stand in.

But more importantly, for Luke anyway, resting on pegs above the fireplace was the most beautiful double-barreled shotgun he'd ever seen. It was a side-by-side 12-gauge with a polished walnut stock on which was a brass plate bearing the name of the manufacturer, James Purdey and Sons, London. Luke loved all guns, but especially shotguns and he was dying to take it down and hold it, so he could feel its perfect balance and admire its fine craftsmanship. But before he could ask Teddy's permission, she pointed at a big guilt-framed painting hanging on the far wall.

'That's Father, right there.' She led him up to the painting which showed a short, dark-haired, beetle-browed West Point cadet astride a magnificent white horse. It took Luke a moment but then he realized it was the same man as the bust in the hall, only much younger. 'Of course,' she added, 'that was painted long before his injury confined him to a wheelchair.'

'An injury,' a voice added, 'that would never have happened if your dear departed mother hadn't encouraged him to take up dressage and show jumping.'

Luke turned and saw an elegant woman standing in the doorway. She wore hand-tailored western clothes and he reckoned her custom cowboy boots cost more than his pawned saddle. She was nearing fifty but still aces. She had premature silver-gray hair cut short like a boy's, almond-shaped jade-green eyes and the kind of chiseled features seen on statues. The only thing that prevented her from being shout-aloud beautiful was her mouth. She had pinched thin lips that seemed to sneer at Luke as if he were inferior.

Beside him, Teddy stiffened and her eyes blazed with hatred.

'Don't you dare talk about Momma that way,' she raged. 'She had nothing to do with Father's injury and you know it. Long before he graduated from the Point, he'd already decided to raise jumpers. And like you and everyone knows, once Father decides to do something, nothing or no one can make him change his mind.'

The woman shrugged, impervious to Teddy's anger, and entered the room. 'If you say so,' she said dismissively. 'Frankly, I wouldn't know anything about your father's stubbornness. In the years we've been married, he's always been sweet, obliging and considerate.'

'That's because somehow, Delores, you've managed to twist him around your little finger.'

'Now, now, dear,' Delores Austin taunted. 'Let's not squabble in front of strangers. Speaking of which, where are your manners, child? Aren't you going to introduce me to your handsome young friend?'

'I'm not a child and he's not my friend,' Teddy snapped. 'He's just someone I hired to replace Grady.'

'You fired Zach Grady?'

'No. He was thrown from his horse and broke his leg.'

'I see. Well, you can still introduce us, can't you?'

Teddy grudgingly obeyed, teeth clenched throughout the introduction.

Delores smiled and shook Luke's hand. Though it was only a handshake, she somehow made it feel so sensual, he became aroused.

'Congratulations,' she needled Teddy. 'It's about time we had some attractive young men around here instead of a bunch of bowlegged old veterans who dribble snuff and have more wrinkles than a dead lizard.'

Before Teddy could reply a tall, thin, proud-looking Mexican with long white hair and a white drooping *pistolero* mustache wheeled in a man whose legs were covered by a blanket. Though only sixty, he looked ten years older. He also looked familiar and after a few moments Luke realized it was the man in the painting.

'What're you two arguing about now?' he demanded. '*Madre de Dios*, can't you two be left alone for a second without fighting!'

'We weren't fighting, dearest,' Delores said, quickly joining her husband. 'On the contrary, Luther, I was congratulating your daughter for hiring someone who isn't old enough to have fought in the Civil War.'

Luke had been studying Teddy's father and could barely believe that the robust, pugnacious-looking West Point cadet had become so withered and frail.

But though he'd lost the use of both legs and could only sit hunched over, hands clasped limply in his lap there was still fire in his eyes as he said to his daughter: 'You hired someone without my say so?'

Stung by his tone, Teddy reddened. 'Isn't that what someone running a ranch is supposed to do when a man goes down? Or have I been demoted without my knowledge?'

Luther Austin broke into a big smile that brought life to his sunken face.

'Some daughter, hey?' he said to Luke. 'I swear to God, nothing makes me prouder than when she spits fire at me.' He motioned for the old *pistolero* to wheel him closer and offered Luke a leathery claw-like hand. 'So you're replacing Zach Grady?'

'I don't know about replacing him, Mr. Austin,' Luke said, shaking hands. 'But you'll get the best I can give. That I promise you, sir.'

'No man can do better, son. Welcome to Shadow Hills.'

'Thank you.' Luke turned to Teddy, adding: 'I'll wait outside.'

She nodded and turned back to her father.

'Before you go, little girl,' he told her, 'get over here and give your daddy a big hug.' He stretched out his arms. Teddy leaned into them and not only hugged him but kissed him fondly on the cheek.

Luke glanced at Delores. She looked jealous enough to kill.

He left the parlor, wondering if he'd stuck his head in a noose by hiring on with these folks. But, what the hell, beggars couldn't be choosers. So Luke vowed to do his job, earn his wages, mind his own business and most important of all, to stay clear of both women. Because much as he liked the ladies, something warned him that if he ever got close to either one of them, or took sides, he was asking for deep trouble.

5

As Luke waited on the porch for Teddy, he overheard several hands talking nearby. Veterans twice his age, they were mending a corral fence. Their backs to him, which was why they hadn't seen him, and they were talking in low voices. He didn't usually eavesdrop, but when he heard his name mentioned he stood behind one of the posts supporting the porch overhang and listened to what they were griping about.

Apparently the bunkhouse was full, which wasn't surprising. Summer and early fall was when the herds of wild mustangs roaming the southwest were rounded up, broken, and sold either to the cavalry or glue factories and most bunkhouses were full. Normally, this wouldn't have been a problem. But in this case the men were worried that

41

Grady might be fired in the morning to make room for Luke. They didn't want that. They liked Grady. He was fun to be around and always earned his keep. He was also one of them, not a stranger who already seemed to be a favorite of their boss, Miss Teddy. This was another problem. Much as they wanted to get rid of the new hire, they couldn't afford to alienate her by making their resentment too obvious or they might also get fired.

It took a while but they finally decided that the best way to protect Grady and themselves was to give Luke the silent treatment and hope that he'd quit.

Luke laughed to himself. Given a choice he preferred being a loner, so he sure as hell wasn't about to walk away from a good-paying job just because no one talked to him.

Teddy now joined him on the porch. She looked pleased with herself. 'I knew Father would take a liking to you, L.C. You're just his type.'

'And what type is that?'

Ignoring his question, she said: 'Until a bunk becomes available, you're to bed down in the barn.'

'I hope that don't mean you're firing Zach Grady.'

'What happens to Zach is none of your damned business,' she snapped. 'You were hired to break mustangs. Nothing else!'

Feeling spanked, Luke vowed to keep his mouth shut from now on.

'While we're on the subject of dos and don'ts,' she continued, her gray eyes narrowing, 'there's something we should get straight right now, L.C.'

'What's that?'

'Never lie to me. I hate liars. Lying's despicable and I won't tolerate it. That clear?'

'Yep.'

'That includes *white* lies from you when you're trying to butter me up.'

'I get it, ma'am.'

'Don't call me ma'am. I don't like it.'

'What should I call you then?'

'Teddy or Miss Teddy, whichever you prefer.'

'Miss Teddy suits me fine.'

'Very well,' she said, softening. 'Now, to finish what I was saying: I've told McClory to give you whatever you need — guns, gear, the mustang of your choice or even a horse from the remuda, if you prefer.'

'Thanks.'

'Is there anything else you want?'

'Nothing I can think of.'

'Good. Because I want you to be content here, both for your sake and mine.'

She sounded pleasant and sincere and unable to keep up with her ever-changing moods, Luke said: 'I'm sure everything will be fine, Miss Teddy.'

'Well, if it isn't or if you're unhappy about something and want to get it off your chest, don't hesitate to come to me. Running a spread this size is difficult even when the men are content. When they're not, it's damned near impossible.'

'You can count on me.'

'I hope so. I consider myself an excellent judge of character and hate it when people prove me wrong; especially with Father breathing down my neck.' She paused, and abruptly turning irritable again, said: 'I swear, L.C., sometimes it's as if he's just waiting for me to fail.'

'I doubt that, Miss Teddy.'

'Oh, why's that?'

'By the way he looked at you when we left him. It's none of my business, but I'd bet the farm that your father loves you dearly.'

'Maybe,' she said, not convinced. 'But if he does, he sure has a strange way of showing it. Anyway,' she continued, 'you're right. It's not your business and I was wrong for bringing it up. You're here to break mustangs, not to listen to me griping. So why don't you get started and prove you're worth those high wages I'm paying you.' She spun around and re-entered the house.

Amazed by her quicksilver moods,

Luke again promised himself that from now on he'd keep his nose out of the family squabbles and just do his job.

As he walked to the corral containing a bunch of unbroken mustangs he passed the veterans fixing the fence. He tried to read their expressions, but they were too guarded. He figured they were so used to Teddy's tirades they were immune to them, treating them like passing thunder storms and then going back to work.

Luke knew if he wanted to stay there he should do the same. But he couldn't. Even though he knew he was courting disaster, he was attracted to Teddy, much like a moth drawn to a flame, and that worried him enough to make him wish he had his own horse. Because then he would have mounted up and ridden clear the hell out of there.

6

Though he wasn't yet thirty, Luke knew as much about breaking broomtails as any wrangler. He also knew that whatever he'd learned about mustangs and wrangling he'd learned from Judd Ames, an old timer who was dead now but at the time was foreman at the *Double S*, Stillman J. Stadtlander's ranch, a huge 200,000-acre spread southeast of Santa Rosa.

Luke was still shy of twenty then and raw as they come — a cocky, smart-mouth drifter wandering from one ranch to another, all the while trying to pass himself off as a veteran wrangler. Judd, who was on the north side of sixty, saw right through Luke and had no qualms about cuffing every lie out of him. But at the same time, he saw enough of himself in Luke not to quit on him, as so many other bosses had done. Instead, he decided that fate had chosen him to be the one to make a man out of Luke.

It was tough love from day one. Judd never abused Luke, but his backside soon became all too familiar with the foreman's belt as he whaled the rebel out of him. A fast learner, once Luke realized he couldn't outfox Judd by pretending to be someone he wasn't, he quit being stubborn and the two of them bonded, like father and son. Daily they spent hours together, often after a full day's work, with Judd patiently teaching Luke the ropes. Judd called this learning process the Three Rs — roping, riding, and relaxing. Luke was a natural when it came to the first two, but had trouble learning to relax. But he stuck at it until he finally caught on. Once that happened, the wild horses responded in kind and from then on Luke was on his way to becoming the wrangler he was today.

As for Judd, he wasn't the kind of man who praised anyone to their face.

It was months in fact before Luke realized that instead of being disappointed in him, as he thought, Judd was actually proud of him. But he hid it well. And Luke might never have known how much Judd thought of him if he hadn't overheard the foreman tell Stadtlander that it was time Luke got a raise. When Stadtlander asked him why, Judd said bluntly: 'Because he's earned it, boss. Oh, sure, the kid's more trouble than a bull in heat, but he's got more talent than any other two men you got drawing wages.'

God, Luke thought as he remembered his moments with Judd, how he loved that old man! He was worth ten real fathers and every night Luke prayed that they'd be together for years. But Judd had demons of his own, and one night he and his old pal Jack Daniels drunkenly wandered out into a rainstorm and were washed away in a flash flood.

Distraught, Luke stayed at the ranch long enough to attend the funeral, then collected his wages and rode off. From that day on, he'd been on his own.

Now, as he reached the corral, Luke knew he had to prove himself to the men in order to win them over. And as more and more of them eagerly gathered along the fence, he studied the mustangs carefully before deciding which one to break first. He finally settled on the meanest mustang in the corral, a wild-eyed red roan stallion that was bullying the other broomtails and entered the corral.

The stallion reacted as he'd expected. Even as Luke closed the gate behind him, it bared its teeth and charged him, forcing him to dive under the fence.

The men howled.

Rising, Luke dusted himself off and re-entered the corral. The other mustangs shied away and huddled nervously in the far corner. Not the stallion. It charged him again. This time Luke held his ground, twirling the knotted end of his rope in front of him in an effort to keep the angry horse at bay. At the same time he spoke soothingly to it, trying to calm it and make it understand that he meant it no harm.

His calmness only increased the mustang's fury. It pounded the dirt with its forelegs and reared up, pawing at the air. Luke still held his ground. Confused by his refusal to run, the stallion dropped down and snorted with rage. Luke stopped twirling his rope but continued to talk to it, trying to gentle it as he inched closer and closer.

The men watching from the fence nodded approvingly. Luke might not be their pal, Grady, their expressions said, but he sure was no stranger to broomtails.

It took a while but finally Luke trapped the foam-flecked red roan mustang in one corner of the corral and by twirling his rope from side-to-side forced it to remain there. It gave a shrill whistling scream and glared at him, wild-eyed, quivering, froth dripping from its open mouth, not sure what to expect next.

That's when Luke spun out a loop.

Twirling it, he threw it over the roan's head and jerked it tight. Instantly all hell broke loose: the panicked mustang reared up, whinnying, pawing at the air and bucking as it tried to break free of the noose.

Keeping the rope taut Luke backed up and quickly wrapped the other end of it around a post in the middle of the corral. He was just in time. The mustang charged him, hooves flying, teeth bared as it tried to bite him, forcing Luke to jump aside or get trampled. But he kept hold of the lariat, leaning back as he braced against the strain, while the stallion raced around the corral in an ever-diminishing circle, the rope wrapping coil after coil about the post.

Finally the rope got so short it jerked the mustang off its feet. Winded, it slowly got up and stood facing Luke, flanks heaving, slathered in sweat, fighting to get its breath. He waited for the stallion to calm down then inched closer, all the while talking soothingly to it.

That's when he heard footsteps behind him. Turning, he saw two of the men approaching. Glad that he'd won them over Luke smiled inwardly and faced front again. Without a word, one man cautiously approached the mustang and grabbed its ear. It tried to bite him but the man punched it on its soft velvety nose and the roan stallion recoiled, shaken. Meanwhile, the other man dropped a blanket and saddle at Luke's feet, grasped the rope and nodded for him to let go.

Grateful, Luke obeyed. Picking up the blanket, he put it on the mustang's back. It trembled but didn't move or try to bite him. He spoke softly to it. It didn't fight him but it did turn its head, watching him with wild inflamed eyes. Sensing he'd temporarily won it over Luke slowly raised the saddle, showed it to the horse and then placed it on its back. The stallion bucked half-heartedly then stood still, quivering as Luke tightened the cinch under its belly. Then gripping the reins, he stepped up into the saddle and clamped his knees against the mustang's flanks.

'Let 'er rip,' he told the two men. They jumped back and ran for the fence.

The mustang didn't disappoint him. Like a tightly wound spring suddenly uncoiling, it arched its back, stiffened all four legs and bucked straight up in the air. For one exhilarating moment Luke felt like he was flying. It was an experience like no other. No matter how often he broke wild horses and thought he knew what to expect next, each experience with each horse always proved him wrong.

Today was no exception. The roan mustang exploded under him and somehow managed in mid-air to twist sideways and arch its back at the same time. Despite the unique move, Luke wasn't thrown. He gripped the reins and tried to ignore the roaring in his ears that loudened with each violent spiraling jump. Time and again he left the saddle only to thump back down again with jarring force. Pain shot up his spine. But he grimly clung on, his boots thrust into the stirrups, knees clamped against the mustang's flanks, trying desperately to stay on its back.

For the next few minutes the angry stallion tested Luke's stamina to its fullest, bucking, fish-tailing and landing stiff-legged, jolting the breath out of him. He felt like he was getting hit with sledgehammers while at the same time his spine seemed ready to snap and his guts threatened to jar loose.

But he refused to quit. And gradually, after several trips around the corral, the bucking slackened off and Luke knew he'd outlasted the gutsy mustang. It gave a final half-hearted buck and then quit. Luke let out a painful, relieved sigh. Under him the exhausted, sweat-lathered broomtail could only stand there, quivering, breathing hoarsely, all the fight drained out of it. Luke cautiously relaxed, knowing that nothing compared to the exhilaration he now felt.

That wasn't all. As he cooled off the

mustang by walking it slowly around the corral, the way the men looked at him told Luke he'd won their respect. He also knew that by nightfall word would have reached Teddy and her father, hopefully earning him the job as boss wrangler until Zach Grady was fit enough to return to work.

McClory was a different story. As Luke dismounted, he saw the surly foreman watching him over the fence. His sour expression hid whatever he was thinking. All Luke could do was guess that for some personal reason McClory wasn't happy with him. It was unsettling, and Luke knew that until they found a way to settle their differences, he was in for a rough time.

7

He broke four more broomtails that day and by suppertime was dog-tired and sore all over. Wearily removing his shirt, he washed up in the water trough behind the barn. Several hands were washing up beside him. They didn't say anything. They didn't have to. Their friendliness told Luke that he was now one of them. And when they walked off to eat supper, he couldn't help but feel vindicated.

As he was toweling off, he heard someone approach. By the lightness of the footsteps he knew it wasn't a man and he turned, hoping to see Teddy.

But it was Delores. With a faintly mocking smile she eyed him up and down like she was undressing him.

'I just wanted to say how wonderful you were out there today,' she cooed. 'I always thought Zach Grady was the best wrangler I'd ever seen, but after watching you, why he couldn't polish your boots.'

Her flattery rolled off Luke's back. She hadn't been among the onlookers and knowing that she was just flirting, he said: 'How would you know, Mrs. Austin? You weren't even watching.'

'Ah, but I was,' she said, indicating an upper window, 'from up there.'

'Oh.'

'You must come up and look for yourself sometime.'

''Mean from your bedroom?'

'Of course,' she said seductively: 'You'd find the view most . . . stimulating.'

He wasn't easily embarrassed. But her tone was so suggestive, he blushed.

'How sweet,' she taunted. 'How quaintly naïve. Obviously, I must be careful what I say to you from now on, L.C. I wouldn't want you to misunderstand me and not know when I'm teasing you.'

Angry at himself, he said: 'Don't worry, Mrs. Austin. I doubt if I'll ever misunderstand you or what you're implying.'

'That's good to know . . . ' She fondly stroked his cheek, again undressing him with her eyes. Then she turned and walked toward the house. Halfway there she stopped and looked back at him. 'Oh, before I forget: until my husband decides whether to fire Grady or not, you're to bunk in the servants' quarters with Rivera.'

'Rivera?'

'Luther's long-time friend and watchdog.'

''Mean that old Mexican who wheels Mr. Austin around?'

'Uh-huh.'

'B-But what about Miss Teddy?'

'What about her?'

'She told me I was to bunk in the barn.'

'Is that so?' Delores smiled, deadly sweet. 'Well, now you've been told differently. And this time by my husband, who just *happens* to own Shadow Hills. So I suggest you do as he says.' She walked off before he could reply.

He watched her. He couldn't help it. She made sure of that. With every slinky step, every suggestive swing of her hips she turned something as innocent as walking into a sexual act.

'You're a damn' fool,' a voice growled behind him.

Startled, Luke whirled around and saw McClory approaching from the barn.

'But I reckon you already know that, don't you, kid — '

'Don't call me kid.'

' — from your vast experiences with other men's wives?'

His sarcasm angered Luke and he was tempted to swing on the foreman. But wanting to keep his job, he controlled his temper and said: 'Everyone's entitled to their own opinion, boss.'

'I knew it when I first laid eyes on you,' McClory said.

'Knew what?'

'That you can't keep your dick in your jeans.'

'So that's what's bothering you,'

Luke said, steamed. 'You can't get it up anymore.'

McClory went white and Luke knew he'd hit pay dirt.

'How'd you like to repeat that in there?' the foreman said, indicating the barn. 'Or are you too yellow to back up your mouth?'

'Why don't we go find out?'

'Not now. Too many eyes.'

'When?'

'Tonight. After supper, when most folks have turned in.'

'I'll be there.' Luke started to walk away then stopped and looked back at him. 'Fists, guns, knives, what?'

'Fists.'

'Perfect,' Luke said. 'I don't have an iron anyway.' Draping the towel around his neck he walked off, feeling McClory's eyes boring a hole in his back.

8

Breaking all those broncs had given Luke a big appetite and an even bigger thirst, but that night he didn't enjoy his supper. He was too busy thinking about his fight with McClory. No matter the outcome, he knew he'd end up losing — either his job or his teeth! And he needed both.

The men were friendly now and as he sat among them at the long table in the grub shack, toying with his ham hocks and greens, he decided to find out all he could about McClory in hope of finding a weakness. He kept his questions casual, so no one would suspect he was pumping them for information, and by the end of the meal knew more than he needed to know about the surly foreman.

McClory was a good man to work for. He was fair, didn't expect the men to do anything that he wouldn't do himself, and always stood up for them when he felt Teddy was driving them too hard. On the negative side, he was moody, short-tempered, held grudges and mostly kept to himself.

Realizing he'd learned nothing that would help him win the fight, Luke was about to drop the subject when one of the veterans, Stumpy Bendix, who had lost an eye during a stampede, said quietly: 'You know, Thad wasn't always like he is now.'

''Mean you've worked for him before?'

'Stumpy fought alongside him in the war,' said Pike Gilman. 'They were in the Second Texas Mounted Rifles, stationed at Fort Clark.'

'Right up till Lee surrendered,' added Brock Cooper. 'Right, Stump?'

Stumpy grunted and began sopping up his beans with a crust.

'So the war changed him?' Luke said. 'That what you're saying?'

Stumpy went on eating for a few

moments, then without looking up, said: 'Not the war. Losing.'

The word brought pain to every southerner around Luke.

'Makes sense,' Pike agreed. 'If sense is what a man's looking for.'

'Looking for it,' Brock said, 'don't mean he's going to find it.'

'Amen, brother.'

'He'd *better* find it,' an outrider said, 'if he ever wants peace of mind.'

'For some men,' said his kid brother, 'peace of mind's even harder to find.'

'If they ever find it at all, that is,' Pike said.

The other hands nodded solemnly as if he'd said something profound.

'You boys can have peace of mind,' joked Curly Nix, a former miner who drove the chuck wagon. 'Me, I'll take a big-hipped, big-titty woman anytime!'

Everyone laughed and continued eating.

But Brock wasn't finished. 'The war ain't all Thad lost,' he said soberly.

'Meaning?' Luke asked.

'When he got mustered out, his wife wasn't waiting for him outside the fort. It cut him deep. He waited for two days, but she never showed. She didn't send no message either, saying why she wasn't there. So Thad, figuring something bad had happened to her or his young'uns, started walking home. He was from southwest Texas — Midland, I think — which was a far piece from Fort Clark and it took him several days to reach his farm. By then he'd worn out his boots and his feet were a mess of blisters. Worse, there was still no sign of his wife or his three littl'uns. Well, as you can imagine, by now the poor bastard was half-crazy with worry. That's when one of his neighbors gave him the news: his wife had run off with a Bible puncher.'

'So much for goddamn white collars,' Curly grumbled.

'She left their young'uns behind, too,' Pike said bitterly, 'without so much as a fare-thee-well or go fend for yourselves.'

'What made it worse,' added Ned Harper, who was an artist with a running iron, 'by the time Thad found the girls, they were dying of Black Water fever.'

'Yeah,' put in Curly, 'and he never did find his son.'

'Most likely died of fever, same as the girls,' said Harper. ''Least, that's what Thad figured.'

'*Jesus*,' Luke said. 'No wonder he's so crusty.'

Everyone at the table nodded in agreement.

'That ain't all,' Harper said. 'Not long after Thad buried his daughters, he ran into a Yankee patrol. They beat him bloody and castrated him with a bayonet. Said there was too many Johnny Rebs running around already.'

'He would've bled to death for sure,' said Curly, 'if some rube farmer hadn't happened to be passing. He put Thad in his wagon and took him to this horse doctor, who sewed Thad up and cared for him till he could walk again.'

'Some folks say that's why he took up bare-knuckle fighting,' Pike said: ' — to get revenge by beating up blue bellies.'

Something cold and clammy dropped in Luke's belly.

'McClory was a prize fighter?'

'Sure,' Pike said. 'Got to be state champion. Didn't you know?'

Suddenly, Luke's throat was too dry to answer.

9

As soon as supper was over, Luke and the men walked to the barn.

McClory was waiting for him just inside the open doors. He was stripped to the waist, wore black pugilist tights tucked into laced-up boots and his muscular upper body glistened menacingly in the lamp-light.

Luke knew then that he was in for a beating. But there was no quit in him. Besides, he knew if he walked away now he'd lose the respect of the men and, more importantly, of Teddy as well and that was unacceptable. So he rolled up his shirt-sleeves and confronted McClory.

The big sour-faced foreman grinned mockingly at him and flexed his muscles. 'Well, well, look who's here?' he taunted. 'I never thought you'd show up, kid. Figured by now you'd be halfway to Texas.'

'Well, you figured wrong, didn't you?' Luke said. 'Only way this fight don't happen is if you call it off.'

McClory gave an ugly laugh. 'Why would I do that, kid? I ain't had the pleasure of beating the chaff out of someone since I quit the ring.'

For the second time that night something cold and clammy sank in Luke's belly.

'Someone call it,' McClory said as they squared off.

'Get at it, you two,' Stumpy obliged.

Fists cocked, McClory started circling Luke.

'What about rules?' Pike said.

'Fair Play rules,' Stumpy said. 'In other words, gents, no kicking, biting or eye-gouging.'

'Suits me,' McClory said.

'Me too,' Luke added. Then, suddenly raising his hand: 'Wait, wait!'

'Jesus,' McClory grumbled, 'what now?'

Luke opened his mouth and took out the bridge holding his two false front teeth. Tucking it in his pocket, he glared at McClory. 'Okay, whale away, damn you!'

'Last man standing wins, kid.'

'Fine,' Luke said and kicked the foreman in the groin.

But McClory was no fool. As if expecting dirty tactics from Luke he spun sideways, his thigh taking most of the kick. Grunting with pain, he staggered back and dropped to one knee. Luke kicked him again, this time in the ribs. McClory gasped, fighting to catch his breath, stumbled and fell down. Luke circled him, waiting until he struggled to his knees and then moved in to finish him off.

It was a mistake.

McClory took Luke's next kick to his belly. But instead of doubling over, as Luke had expected, the foreman grabbed the young wrangler's foot and twisted, throwing him off-balance. Luke went down hard, head bouncing off the floor, lights exploding before his eyes and blacked out.

When he came around, McClory was on his feet and had him by the shirt front. Jerking Luke up, he slammed him against the post. Luke's head snapped back and struck the lamp hanging there. Dazed, he lurched forward into a looping roundhouse right that knocked him sprawling. His head hit the floor and for the second time he blacked out.

He had no idea how long he lay there. But the next thing he remembered he was being pummeled in the belly. Gasping for breath, he sank to his knees, his jaw exposed to a huge uppercut. It exploded under his chin, mercifully putting Luke to sleep and ending all his pain.

10

Cold water splashing over his face brought Luke around. For a few moments everything looked blurred. Then as the fog cleared, he realized he was on his knees with McClory standing over him, fists cocked, an empty bucket at his feet.

'Welcome back, kid,' he said, grinning. 'Ready for round two?'

Luke ignored the voice inside his head warning him to keep quiet, and said:

'Up yours.' He then closed his eyes, expecting more punishment.

But nothing happened. He opened his eyes and found McClory eying him with curious respect.

'Go ahead, damn you,' Luke said. 'Pound away to your heart's content. Ain't nothing you can do that every broomtail I've broke ain't already done and better.'

McClory was tempted, but something stopped him and he unclenched his fists. 'You're one tough *hombre*,' he admitted. 'I'll give you that, kid.'

'Don't call me kid.'

'Then tell me your name.'

'You know my name — L.C.'

'Your real name.'

So there it was again. But this time it didn't embarrass Luke. Maybe it was the beating or the pain in his belly or maybe even the pounding ache in his head that threatened to blow his ears off, but suddenly he didn't give a damn anymore and said defiantly: 'I ain't got a real name.'

'Don't prod me, kid. Everybody's got a real name.'

'I don't.'

'Then what does L.C. stand for?'

Luke swallowed hard. 'Lost Cause.'

McClory scowled. 'Don't jerk my tail, boy, or I'll beat you bloody.'

'I ain't jerking your tail, and that's for true.'

'Then tell me why you don't have a name.'

'What's the point? You won't believe me.'

73

'Try me.'

Luke thought back to the orphanage and the harsh but fair treatment he'd received from Sister Ines and the other nuns. Most of the time he was able to block all those years out, but occasionally, like now, they came back to haunt him.

'I said, try me,' McClory repeated.

Trapped, Luke said: 'Okay, if you want to know the truth, I barely knew my folks. I never met my pa. He was in the army and stationed in Texas.'

McClory looked interested. 'Where in Texas?'

'I don't remember,' Luke said.

'What about your ma?'

'The only thing I remember about her is, she was always locking me in the closet while she entertained one of my so-called uncles.'

'Mother Mary,' McClory said, even more interested. 'By any chance do you remember her name?'

'Rosalie, I think it was. 'Least that's what all her men visitors called her.'

McClory reacted as if the name meant something to him, but didn't say what. Mind churning, he said only: 'Go on.'

Luke shrugged. 'Well, one day, while I was locked in the closet, one of the uncles beat Ma bloody. The next morning her face was all swollen and she could barely walk, but she got dressed and took me to El Paso. There she left me on the doorstep of this chapel that was part of an orphanage. She promised to be right back, but that was the last time I saw her. So the nuns took me in and since there was no note pinned on me saying who I was, Sister Ines, who was in charge, named me Joseph. But even though I liked her and she was nicer to me than the other nuns, I wouldn't answer to it, or any of the other Biblical names she called me. So she finally gave up and from then on everyone just called me 'child'. Not that I gave a hoot. Having a name wouldn't have changed nothing. I hated being there and wouldn't do as I was told, no matter how often they whipped me or sent me to bed without my supper — which was why in the end they decided I was a lost cause and sent me to reform school. There, when the Matron asked me my name, I said the first thing that came to my head and told her it was L.C. She asked me what the initials stood for. I didn't want to say 'lost cause', so I said I didn't know. She believed me and after that, everyone called me L.C.'

While Luke had been talking, he noticed that McClory's expression had changed from interest to curiosity to what seemed like, incredulous disbelief.

'I ain't lying if that's what you're thinking,' Luke assured him. 'Every word I've told you is the God's honest truth.'

McClory stared at him but didn't speak for the longest time. Though his expression never changed, his eyes did. They seemed to reflect all the different thoughts that were racing through his mind. It was as if he was trying to grapple with something Luke had said, something that he desperately wanted to believe but was just too much of a stretch for him to accept, and finally he gave up and said: 'Go clean up, kid.'

'Dammit, I asked you not to call me kid.'

'Would you sooner I called you Lost Cause?'

'I'd *sooner* you called me L.C. And that's for true.'

McClory snorted, 'For true, you say?' and expelled his frustration in an explosive sigh. 'What in seven hells do you know about the truth, boy?'

'Only what I just told you.'

'Told me? *Told* me? Ha! You don't *know* what you've told me. You don't even have the vaguest clue.'

He was right and Luke didn't contradict him.

'Thanks to you, kid, I've now got to deal with a bunch of skeletons that I never knew existed before.'

'Skeletons? What skeletons?'

'Ramifications, kid. Consequences

dragged up from the past.'

'I still don't know what you're talking about, boss.'

''Course you don't. Hell, you don't even know the *half* of it.'

'Half of what?'

'The truth, by God! The whole, sordid, painful goddamn truth!'

'About what?' Luke demanded angrily. 'Quit talking in riddles and tell me!'

But McClory was past explaining anything. Frustrated by whatever was troubling him, he grabbed his shirt and stormed out before Luke could say another word.

11

Because Luke was bunking with Rivera in the servants' quarters, the men didn't see him till the next morning at breakfast. By then they had already seen McClory's skinned knuckles and putting two-and-two together, didn't heckle Luke about his bruises. Grateful, he ate his grub in silence. He felt like he'd been run over by the chuck wagon. But he had broncs to break, so he hobbled to the corral.

There, later, he ran into Teddy. She gasped as she saw his battered face and demanded to know what had happened.

Luke shrugged and said: 'All part of the job, Miss Teddy.'

'Don't give me that, L.C. I want to know exactly how you got hurt.'

'That's easy. I got stomped.'

'By one of the mustangs?'

'Yeah. That big gray stallion you like.'

'When?'

'Yesterday, while I was breaking him.'

'Really?' She eyed him doubtfully. 'Looks more like you were in a fight.'

'Why would I get into a fight?'

'That's what I want to know.'

'There's nothing to know. I didn't get into no fight. 'Least, not with anything that walks on two legs.'

She still wasn't convinced. 'Would you tell me if you *had* been fighting?'

'Sure. But that ain't what happened, Miss Teddy — though I wish it had.'

'What do you mean?'

'I've had my fair share of fights and believe me fists don't hurt near as bad as that gray's hooves.' Tipping his hat, he opened the gate and entered the corral.

'Wait.'

Luke turned and looked at her.

'Do you think you might feel better by tonight?'

'I sure hope so. Why?'

'Father wants you to join us for dinner.'

80

Surprised, Luke said: 'That's neighborly of him. Mind if I ask why?'

'Because I asked him to.'

Floored, Luke didn't know what to say.

'Of course, if you don't want to come — '

'No, no, I do,' he insisted. 'What time?'

'Seven. And please, don't be late. Father hates tardiness.'

'Don't worry. I ain't about to give Mr. Austin any reason to hate me.'

12

The day dragged by. The sun crawled across the sky like a fly trapped in molasses and each broomtail Luke broke seemed meaner than the one before. He tried to focus on what he was doing, but his mind kept wandering back to Teddy and he was lucky he didn't get busted up or even killed.

He was bucked off a few times, though. He didn't break any bones, which was a miracle, but the final time he was thrown was by a mean-assed dun that was bent on killing him. It threw Luke off into the corral gate and then lunged at him, trying to bite him. Luke smelled its hot sour breath wash over him. He tried to roll aside but was too dazed to move. The dun reared up in a blind rage, intending to stomp him to death.

That's when Pike and another young

wrangler, Kip Frawley, saved Luke's life. They were in the midst of unloading hay from a wagon and happened to see the dun attacking him. Dropping their pitchforks, they rushed over, reached under the gate and dragged Luke to safety.

Before he could thank them, McClory approached and angrily wagged his finger in Luke's face. 'What the hell's wrong with you, kid? You aiming to get yourself killed?'

'No, boss.'

'Then get your head screwed on straight, dammit, or I'll give Kip your job and tell Miss Teddy to hand you your walking papers! The same goes for the rest of you,' he told Pike and the other hands. 'Get back to work or draw your wages!'

As they hurried off, McClory turned back to Luke and in a more friendly tone, said: 'Just so you know, kid, I backed up the story you told Miss Teddy about being stomped by that gray mustang.'

Surprised but grateful, Luke said:

'Thanks, boss. And don't worry none. I won't get tossed no more.'

'I'm glad to hear that,' McClory said, adding: 'About last night, L.C. I was wrong for pounding on you. You didn't deserve it.'

'Sure I did. You're the head honcho and I shouldn't have sassed you.'

'Maybe so, but I still shouldn't have lost my temper like that.' He offered Luke his hand. 'Hope you won't hold it against me.'

'Forget it,' Luke said, shaking his hand. 'I have.'

'Good,' McClory said. 'Now get back to work, okay?' He walked off.

84

13

That evening Luke washed up extra carefully, shaved and slicked his hair back, put on his one clean shirt and best pair of jeans, and started to leave the room he shared with Manuel Rivera. The old *pistolero*, who seldom spoke to him, for some reason decided to step out of character and in stilted but perfect English, told Luke not to accept *Senorita* Teddy's invitation. He added that it was not Luke's place to break bread with either her or her father, '*El Patron*,' and could only lead to trouble or worse, get him fired.

Luke sensed Rivera was right. But he liked Teddy too much to take the old *pistolero's* advice and left. However, as he climbed the steps to the main floor, he argued with himself: one half called him a damned fool for thinking that a rich cultured girl like Teddy, who could have any man she wanted, really cared about him and wasn't just amusing herself with her new hire, while the other half told him to trust his feelings and the way he sensed Teddy felt about him and to think of her invite as a stepping stone to his future.

On reaching the top of the stairs, Luke found the butler waiting for him. A pompous old man with thinning white hair, bristly eyebrows and a white goatee, he had a sneering disdain for any of the hired hands and treated them with contempt. His attitude riled Luke. But before he could say anything he'd later regret, he reminded himself of Sister Ines' last words as she sadly turned him over to the constable from the reform school.

'Always remember, my child, those who listen to Satan end up in hell; only God can invite us into Heaven.'

In other words, Luke thought as the constable locked him in the paddy wagon, he only had himself to blame for what happened to him. Well, so what? Hell was where all his pals were going to end up, so why would he want to be a stranger in heaven?

Now, as the butler led him into the dining-room, Luke saw that Teddy and her father were already seated at the table. A wagon-wheel chandelier of candles hung from the ceiling. His entry caused the flames to flicker, casting eerie shadows on the snowy tablecloth.

Wondering why Delores wasn't there, Luke politely bid Teddy and her father good evening and let the butler seat him. Old Man Austin, who sat hunched over in his wheelchair at the head of the table, looked more pathetically shriveled than usual. He wore a black western suit, starched white shirt and black string tie clasped by a large opal that blazed like fire, and despite the hot water bottle squeezed behind his back kept shivering.

'I'm sorry that my wife couldn't join us,' he said to Luke. 'But I fear she's not feeling well. However, she sent her regrets and hoped you enjoyed your meal.'

'Don't bother to explain, Father,' Teddy said, flaring. 'I'm sure L.C. more than understands Delores' absence.'

Luke didn't, but felt obliged to say: 'Of course, sir. I'm just grateful you thought of inviting me.'

For a moment Austin looked confused and gave Teddy a sidelong glance that made her laugh.

'Don't worry, Father. I already told L.C. that I asked you to invite him.'

He smiled, as if amused by her admission and shrugged helplessly at Luke.

'There's something you will learn if you ever have daughters, Mr. — uh?'

'L.C.,' Teddy reminded.

'Ah, yes, L.C. — and that is, God can be a practical joker. And one of His jokes on men is He lets us think we rule the roost. But of course, in reality, as every woman knows, we're merely putty in their manipulative hands.'

'Father,' Teddy chided playfully, 'I resent being called manipulative.'

'Cunning?'

'Even worse.'

'Persuasive?'

She laughed. 'I can live with persuasive. Now,' she said to Luke, 'will you please lead us in grace?'

'Happily,' he said. They all bowed their heads and Luke quietly thanked God for the food they were about to eat. As he started to say amen, a kerosene lamp crashed through the window. Shattering on the floor, it burst into flames that quickly spread over the Navaho rug that encircled the table like a colorful island.

Teddy gave a startled scream, while her father fearfully huddled down in his wheelchair and looked at the broken window as outside gunfire broke out. It was followed by horses galloping away and men shouting excitedly.

By now Luke had already grabbed the crystal pitcher and dumped the water over the flames. They hissed and sizzled but defiantly kept burning. Luke ran to the window, tore down one of the maroon drapes and started beating out the fire.

Behind him the butler and Rivera rushed in. Following Luke's lead, they pulled down the other drapes and between the three of them they managed to beat out the flames. By now the room was filled with smoke and everyone was coughing and fighting to breathe. Rivera pushed open another window and as the smoke thinned out, Luke saw that the barn was on fire.

Teddy, who was hovering protectively over her father, let Rivera take her place and smiled gratefully at Luke. But before she could thank him, McClory rushed in, exclaiming: 'They got away, Mr. Austin!'

'Who was it, do you know?'

'I'm not sure, sir. But Pike claims it was Cody Webber and his two boys.'

'Why?' Teddy asked. 'Did he see their faces?'

'No, miss. It's almost dark and besides, they were wearing masks.'

'Then how did Pike — ?'

'He found this on the ground after they'd ridden away.' McClory held up a shiny, round, rope-edged silver concho bearing a Christian cross.

'What's that got to do with the Webbers?' Teddy said. 'Most of our boys have conchos on their saddles and bridles.'

'Not to mention me and half the desert riders in New Mexico,' Luke added.

'Maybe so, but ... ' McClory hesitated.

'Go on, Thad, finish what you were saying.'

'Well, it's true. Most of our hands *do* have conchos on their gear, but none of them have a cross on them. On top of that, Mr. Austin, it ain't no secret how religious the Webbers are. If anybody would have a concho with a cross on it, it'd be them.'

'Let me see that,' Teddy said.

McClory handed her the concho.

She inspected it carefully before saying: 'You absolutely sure about this, Thad? Because if you're wrong, we'll be the laughing stock of the whole valley.'

'I'd stake my life on it,' McClory said. 'But if it'd make you feel better, Miss Teddy, take a look for yourself.'

'I'd like to do that,' she told her father.

'Go ahead,' he said. Then to Luke: 'Go with her, son. Look out for her. And remember, both of you, we're dealing with a widower here, a father of two boys who recently lost their mother and has everyone's sympathy, so be damned sure you don't make any mistakes or overlook anything!'

14

Luke and Teddy discovered that McClory was right: none of the hands at Shadow Hills had crosses on their conchos. Satisfied, Teddy told the foreman to have the men saddle up and be ready to ride.

Luke, thinking that included him, started for the corral. But she grabbed his arm, saying: 'You stick with me! Father values your opinion and I want you to back me up when I tell him we're going after the Webbers.'

'I ain't sure that's a good idea, Miss Teddy. It's growing dark and — '

'I wasn't asking for your opinion,' she snapped. 'Just your support.'

Luke fell silent and accompanied her to the house.

He hadn't believed Teddy when she said her father valued his opinion. But he was wrong. Once they were in the parlor and she'd explained that McClory was right about the men's conchos not having crosses, Austin turned to Luke and said: 'I know you don't know the Webbers, son, but trust me when I tell you that they've been a thorn in my side for years and this is just the last of many run-ins I've had with them.'

'Father's right,' agreed Teddy. 'As far back as I can remember they were always stirring up trouble between us and our neighbors.'

'Not only that,' her father said, 'Cody even got the law involved on one occasion, by telling lies about how I was trying to force all the homesteaders out of the valley. When that didn't work, he and his sons poisoned some of their own cattle and blamed me for it. Can you imagine that — me, a rancher of my status, being accused of poisoning a water hole? The same water hole, I might add, from which my own cattle drank? My God, it's too preposterous to even imagine!' He shook his head in disgust before adding: 'Fortunately, the lawyers I hired were able to prove the whole thing was nothing but a trumped-up fallacy and the judge tossed the case out of court. But that didn't make up for the time, effort and money I wasted defending myself — not to mention the ill will it caused among the other sod busters and some of the businessmen in Santa Rosa.'

'That's exactly why I want to go after the Webbers, Father,' Teddy said.

'You mean now?'

'Yes. Now.'

'But it's almost dark,' he said, echoing Luke's concern.

'I know,' Teddy said. 'But I'll have the men carry torches so we can follow the Webbers' tracks. They can't be too far ahead of us and if we leave now, I know we'll catch up to them. Please, Father,' she begged. 'Let me do this. I guarantee we'll catch the Webbers. And when we do, I'll make sure they're held account-able for not only tonight's incident, but all the other times they've harassed us.'

Her father digested her words and then turned to Luke. 'I know you're new here, L.C., and would be perfectly within your rights if you refused to get involved in this kind of vigilantism. But I'm asking you as a personal favor to ride with my daughter and protect her.'

'Father, I don't need — '

He silenced her with a wave of his hand and turned back to Luke. 'She means the world to me and, frankly, I've lost faith in McClory. He no longer seems to have that shoot-first-and-to-hell-with-the-consequences attitude anymore — an attitude, incidentally, that made me hire him in the first place. In those days, the man was a veritable firebrand! But now — well, to put it bluntly, I can't trust him. He's gone soft. So will you protect my little girl?'

'Father — ' Teddy protested.

'Hush now,' he said. Then to Luke: 'I'm a wealthy man, L.C. You do this for me and I'll see you never want for anything.'

The idea that Old Man Austin thought he could buy his loyalty angered Luke.

'Sir, if I agree it won't be because of any reward, and that's for true. I'll go because I like Miss Teddy enough to want to protect her and see that no harm comes to her.'

'Is that a yes or a no?' Austin demanded.

Luke turned to Teddy. 'You okay with me going along?'

She nodded and gave him a smile that torched his soul.

'Count me in,' Luke told her father.

'Good. Then you have my blessing, Teddy.'

'Thank you, Father. I promise that you won't regret — ' She broke off as the door opened and McClory stuck his surly face in, saying: 'We're waiting on you, Miss Teddy.'

'Be right there, Thad.' She moved close to her father, bent over and kissed him fondly on his pale wrinkled forehead. 'I'll be back soon.'

He nodded, grabbed her hand and clutched it as if he never wanted to let go. 'May God ride with you, daughter!'

Teddy smiled, pleased by her father's concern, and said: 'He always does, Father.' She motioned for Luke to follow her and they both hurried out.

15

Teddy stopped when they reached the front door. 'Thanks for standing up for me back there, L.C. It doesn't happen very often around here and I appreciate it more than you know.'

Compliments always made Luke feel ill-at-ease and this was no exception. 'I didn't do nothing you wouldn't have done for me, Miss Teddy.'

She wasn't listening. Looking toward the parlor, as if still seeing her father, she said bitterly: 'He always wanted a son, you know. It meant more to him than anything else in the world. Oh, he denies it, of course. Especially if I ever mention it or remind him that having a daughter was the biggest disappointment in his life. But it's still true and we both know it. So did Momma when she was alive. What's more, in his own not-so-subtle way Father never lets me forget it. Not for a single second. No matter what I do, what I say or how I handle things, it's never good enough for him. It's never how his 'son' would have handled it.'

'Miss Teddy,' Luke began, 'I don't think — '

'I'm being fair?' She gave a disgusted, hollow laugh. 'That's what everyone says. But they aren't me. They don't live here, under his thumb, being manipulated like a puppet on strings. Because if they did, if they had to listen to him reminding me in a million different little ways, all of them hurtful, that I'm only a girl . . . well, they'd see things differently . . . would see *me* differently.' She broke off suddenly, as if remembering something, and said: 'I'm sorry. What were you going to say?'

Luke had intended to say that he didn't want to get involved in the family affairs but it was too late, so he shrugged and said: 'Nothing.'

'No, really, what was it?'

'If we want to run down the Webbers,

Miss Teddy, I reckon we ought to get started.'

'Yes,' she said, his words jerking her back to the present. 'You're right. We should.' And opening the door, she hurried out.

16

One of the men at the ranch was a big, solemn half-breed named Charley Buffalo. Pale-skinned compared to other Indians, he had his Swedish mother's blue eyes and his Kiowa father's oily black hair, which he always kept braided.

All the men liked Charley. He was even-tempered, honorable, and his dry sense of humor always made them laugh. He was also the best tracker Luke had ever been around. The men joked that he could track a mosquito over rocks and no one doubted it — Teddy included. Once everyone was mounted and ready to leave, she sent Charley ahead to pick up the Webbers' tracks.

Though it was almost dark and drifting clouds often hid the moon, the men carrying torches lighted the way and they all rode at a steady pace.

Everyone was in a grim mood and there was no talking.

Luke had never met the Webbers. But he'd heard the men talking about them, and from what they said it didn't seem like Cody or his two sons were the troublemakers that Teddy and Old Man Austin claimed they were. But orders were orders, and Luke couldn't deny they'd set the barn on fire or tossed a lamp through the parlor window, so he kept quiet and rode next to Teddy, ready to protect her from any harm.

After an hour or so, they reached one of the many narrow, steep-sided ravines that led into the foothills. Charley Buffalo was kneeled at the entrance, torch in hand as he examined the hard-packed dirt for hoof-prints.

He stood up as the riders approached and pointed at the ground. 'They went this way, Miss Teddy.'

'All three of them?'

Charley nodded.

'They must be planning to hole up in the hills.'

'Looks like.'

'Any idea how far ahead they are?'

'Twenty minutes . . . maybe less.' Her questioning look made him point at some scattered horse droppings. 'It's still moist, Miss Teddy. Much longer than that, it'd be dried out.'

'Good work, Charley.'

'Want me to keep looking, miss?'

'Yes, but keep a sharp eye out. I don't want the Webbers using you for target practice.'

McClory, quiet until now, said: 'Maybe we should send someone with him, Miss Teddy. It ain't just the Webbers Charley's got to worry about — there's also Comanches and Comancheros to reckon with once he gets into the hills.'

He was referring to a bunch of lawless white men who made a living selling horses, firearms, ammunition and other goods — all stolen by Comanches in return for cheap firewater — to Mexican ranchers across the border. They were ruthless killers who controlled the Indians by keeping them drunk, and everyone in the valley knew how dangerous it was to enter the hills, especially at night.

'Good thinking,' Teddy said. 'Take three men and stay close to Charley.'

McClory nodded and turned to the men. 'You heard Miss Teddy. Who wants to go with me?'

No one responded. The Comancheros had killed and tortured enough people to make it clear what would happen to anyone they caught.

'Fine,' McClory said. 'Reckon it's just you and me, Charley.'

The contempt in his voice cut deep. Shamed, Stumpy Bendix, Pike Gilman and Brock Cooper grudgingly held up their hands.

'Well now, ain't that sweet?' McClory said. 'Reckon we got some heroes among us after all.'

17

As Charley and his escort rode off, Teddy turned to the remaining men. 'All of you stay alert. Mr. Webber was a sniper during the war. If you see any sign of movement among the rocks or on the ridges, pass the word. Could save a life.'

With Luke riding beside Teddy, they rode in single file into the dark narrow ravine. A prehistoric river had carved its way through what had once been an escarpment, forming towering, sheer-sided cliffs of red sandstone; now, millions of years later the dry sandy riverbed muffled the sound of the horses' hooves.

It was eerily quiet. On both sides the clifftops were often so close together they hid the moon as it drifted between the clouds. Whenever that happened, it became so dark that despite the torches no one could see more than a few yards ahead. Worse, the torches were dangerously close to dying out and Luke knew that without them it was only a matter of time before one of the horses stepped into a hole and broke its leg. He glanced at the men. By their tight-lipped expressions he guessed that some of them already regretted coming along.

He'd never been in any of the ravines and deep canyons that led into the hills bordering the valley. Now, as he rode alongside Teddy, Luke realized the steep cliffs were peppered with natural caves and crevices, each one offering a perfect hiding place from which a shooter could kill any pursuer. He didn't see anyone, but the whole time he had a strange sense that they were being watched. He blamed it on his nerves. But he still kept looking upward, checking every threatening hiding place and vantage spot in the cliffs looming above them.

After a mile or so the ravine ended. Its jagged walls abruptly descended until they flattened out and became part of the open scrubland that was flanked by low rolling hills. They were now in Comanchero territory. And though it was night, when supposedly Indians wouldn't fight for fear of their soul losing its way, Luke knew differently. Soldiers, scouts and Texas Rangers had told him stories of being attacked at night by Kiowas, Tonkawas and Comanches, while newspapers often described how home-steaders and even miners were driven from their shacks by flaming arrows that according to one man, 'lit up the night so brightly we could see the war paint on the faces of the braves.'

The other men must have also felt as uneasy, because once they were out in the open they instinctively closed ranks and formed a tight-knit group about Teddy. If she was nervous, she didn't show it as she turned to Luke and said calmly: 'We should've seen their torches by now — the Webber's, I mean.'

'Unless they've burned out, like ours will do soon.'

'It's possible. Either that or — '

He stopped her. 'If the Webbers have been attacked by the Comancheros, Miss Teddy, we would have heard shooting by now.'

'Yes, I guess so.' She nibbled her lip. It was the first sign of nervousness Luke had seen from her and he admired the way she was holding up.

Ahead, the trail curved around a large rocky outcrop that hid what was beyond it. The rocks were huge, some bigger than a covered wagon, their sides worn smooth by the endless desert winds. Many were piled on top of each another, like massive building blocks, while others had fallen over and lay scattered on the ground. Most of the men had seen the rocks before and one man jokingly described them as: '*Patio de los gigantes!*'

Knowing he meant, 'Playground of the giants,' everyone laughed — then stopped as they heard distant gunfire.

'Hold it!' Teddy barked.

Luke and the men reined up and pulled out their rifles.

They waited, listening intently, but there was no more shooting.

'We've got to help Thad and the others,' Teddy exclaimed. 'They could be pinned down!'

'First, let's see what's on the other side of these rocks,' Luke cautioned.

'But what if — ?'

'Dammit, Miss Teddy, the Webbers or Comancheros might be waiting to ambush us. If we go rushing into their trap, we could all be killed!'

Stung, she glared at him. 'For a noncommittal man, L.C., you're certainly quick to take charge.'

'Would you sooner I kept quiet and let everyone die?'

She flushed, but managed to control her anger. 'What do you suggest?'

'Follow my lead.' He urged his horse forward, keeping to the trail as it curved around the rocks. Teddy and the men followed him, rifles cocked and ready. Most of the torches were now burned out and with the moon hidden behind drifting clouds it was difficult to see more than a short distance in any direction.

Finally, they rounded the rocks. There was nothing threatening on the trail ahead, merely open land, and everyone heaved a grateful sigh.

But their relief was short-lived. Shortly, there was another burst of shooting in the darkness ahead. It was closer than before and this time it was followed by the sound of galloping horses.

'Stay behind me,' Luke told Teddy. Before she could argue, he signaled to the men to stay with her and then rode out in front of them.

18

The sound of the horses was close now and Luke could tell the unseen riders were galloping straight for him. Stopping in the middle of the trail, he levered a round into his Winchester and waited for them to appear.

It wasn't long before they came charging out of the darkness. They were in a group and without the moon all he could see were their silhouettes. He counted at least four or five riders and unable to identify them raised his rifle, ready to shoot if it turned out to be the Webbers or Comancheros.

It wasn't either. As the horsemen got closer, the moon slid from behind the clouds and Luke quickly recognized them.

'Hold your fire!' he told Teddy and the men. 'It's McClory and the boys.'

Teddy said something he didn't

catch. Next thing he knew she and the men came busting past him. He yelled for her to stop but she ignored him and continued riding toward McClory. Cursing, he dug his spurs into the buckskin. The startled horse launched itself and with a few strides was running flat out.

'What the hell you doing?' he shouted as he caught up with Teddy.

'Going to help them,' she yelled, 'in case Comancheros are after them!'

Knowing he couldn't stop her, Luke whipped the buckskin into a dead run and tried to see over its outstretched head if any Comancheros or Comanches were pursuing McClory and his companions.

There weren't. But as the two groups met and everyone reined up, Luke realized Charley Buffalo was missing. He also saw a Comanche war arrow sticking out of the rump of Pike Gilman's horse and immediately feared the worst.

So did Teddy. 'Where's Charley?' she asked McClory.

'He's dead, Miss Teddy. 'Least, I hope he is.'

'What do you mean?'

'He took two arrows in the back, and last we saw he wasn't moving.'

'Mean you just left him there?' Luke said, incredulous.

'What were we supposed to do — get killed trying to save a dead man?'

'*If* he was dead.'

McClory flinched as if he'd been slapped and turned to the three men who had accompanied him. 'Was Charley dead or not?'

'Sure looked like he was dead,' Stumpy Bendix said.

'How the hell would you know?' Luke said angrily. 'You only got one goddamn eye and you can barely see out of that one.'

'Easy, mister,' Pike cautioned. 'Wasn't like we had all day to see if Charley was still breathing.'

'Damn right,' Brock Cooper agreed. 'Them red devils jumped us 'fore we knew it.'

'They were all around us,' Pike added to Teddy. 'Must've been twenty of them, shooting at us from behind the rocks and bushes.'

'What's worse,' Stumpy said, 'by then our torches was almost burned out, so we couldn't see them but they sure as hell could see us.'

'That's the Gospel truth,' said McClory. 'I swear, Miss Teddy, there were arrows coming at us from all directions. Hell, the way them Comanches were swarming around us, it's lucky we weren't all killed.'

The three men with him nodded. At the same time they wouldn't look Teddy in the eye, and Luke knew damned well they felt guilty for deserting a friend.

Teddy considered what she'd just been told then turned to Luke. 'What do you think? Should we go back and see if Charley's really dead or continue looking for the Webbers?'

'It's your call, Miss Teddy. But if it was up to me, and I wanted to sleep nights, I'd make sure Charley wasn't

114

staked out over hot coals, begging his Creator to take him to the Happy Hunting Grounds.'

She nodded, agreeing with him, and said to the men: 'I can't order you to go, boys. Working for wages doesn't include risking your life, no matter what's at stake. But I'm going, and so is L.C., and any one of you who wants to come along is surely welcome. What's more, I'll give any man who does a month's wages.'

The men stirred in their saddles and murmured among themselves.

'We're wasting valuable time,' Teddy said. 'C'mon, L.C.'

'Wait a minute,' Luke said, grabbing her bridle. 'You ain't going.'

'Try and stop me!'

'Dammit, Miss Teddy, I promised your pa I'd protect you and I intend to keep that promise.'

'That's all the more reason for you to come with me, L.C. But whether you do or don't, I'm still going.' She kicked up her horse, jerking the bridle from his hand, and galloped on along the trail.

Cursing her pig-headedness, Luke dug his spurs in and rode after her.

It was an impulsive act and one he hoped he wouldn't regret. It was then he heard hoof beats coming up behind him. It was a welcome sound. Turning, he saw the men spurring their horses after him and silently thanked them for their courage and loyalty.

19

As they rode deeper into the dark hills, Luke heard tom-toms beating. He guessed it was the Comanches celebrating their victory over the White Eyes. At the same time he visualized Charley Buffalo praying for death as he writhed over hot coals. It was a lousy image and Luke whipped the buckskin to make it go faster.

Using the drums to guide them, they left the trail and rode hard in an easterly direction. All the torches had now burned out. But as if to help them find Charley, the moon obligingly came from behind the clouds to light their way.

The sound of the tom-toms grew louder, warning them that they were getting close. They slowed their horses to a walk, ever watchful for danger. On both sides of them the shadowy brown hills began angling toward one another. Eventually, after another mile or so, the lower slopes came together to form a natural sheltered clearing. A glow came from it. Guessing it was from the Comancheros' camp fires, Luke signaled for Teddy and the men to rein up.

'What's your plan?' she asked him as they gathered together.

He didn't have one. But he wasn't about to undermine her trust in him, so pointing at some boulders scattered on a hillside overlooking the campsite, he said: 'Once we reach that hill, everybody dismount and take cover behind those rocks.'

'Then, what?'

'Depends on how many braves we're facing and whether or not Charley's dead or alive.'

'Go on.'

'If he's alive, we start shooting no matter how many there are.'

'And if he's dead?'

'Then we should count heads and if we're badly outnumbered, decide if it's worth risking our necks just to wipe out some Comancheros.'

'Fair enough,' Teddy said. Then to McClory and the men: 'Any questions?'

'Just one,' said McClory. 'Is L.C. giving the orders now?'

'Do you have a problem with that, Thad?'

'No, Miss Teddy. I just want to know who's dealing, that's all.'

'Well, now you know,' she said, adding: 'Let's ride, boys!'

20

It didn't take long to reach the foot of the hill overlooking the Comancheros' camp. Dismounting, Luke, Teddy and the men scrambled up the slope and hid behind the rocks.

Below them in the sheltered clearing the firelight revealed their worst fears: Charley Buffalo was indeed held captive and though he wasn't spread-eagled over hot coals, he was stripped naked, tied to a dead tree stump and arrows had been shot into him. If that wasn't brutal enough, the Comanches had deliberately missed his vital organs so that he would live longer, and blood was still streaming from his wounds. His head was slumped forward, hiding his face, while his limp body sagged against the rope. He wasn't moving and Luke prayed that he was dead. But he wasn't about to leave anything to chance.

He counted how many men they were up against and realized Pike was right: there were twenty of them — four slovenly, unwashed, bearded Comancheros, all heavily armed, and sixteen wild-eyed drunken Comanches. The white men were drinking by the fire, laughing and egging on the braves who were dancing around Charley to the beat of the tom-toms. Empty whiskey bottles lay everywhere. Luke scanned the camp, looking for additional weapons, and saw the braves' rifles piled on their blankets behind the Comancheros.

Turning to Teddy and the men crouched behind the rocks, he motioned to them to start firing on his signal. They nodded to show they understood and cocked their rifles.

Luke sighted in on one of the braves dancing around Charley's corpse, dropped his hand and pulled the trigger. The roar of his Winchester was hidden as Teddy and the men opened fire. They all had repeating rifles that held fifteen cartridges and the firing seemed to go on forever.

Luke pumped round after round into the hapless braves. It was like shooting clay pigeons at a fair. Soon, dead and dying Comanches lay everywhere. The remaining braves stopped dancing and drunkenly staggered to their rifles.

They never made it. Luke and the others gunned them down. They then shot the four white Comancheros as they ran for cover. Three of them died without even drawing their guns; the fourth man staggered on for a few steps and then collapsed.

But that wasn't the end of it. Luke, Teddy and the men shot the Comanches who'd been beating the drums and, lastly, the wounded.

The slaughter was finally over. Luke felt no shame for killing unarmed men and doubted if anyone else did either. The Comancheros had tortured and killed Charley Buffalo, a fine man and a good friend, and as Luke accompanied Teddy and the men down the hillside to the corpses he felt a sense of satisfaction that only came with payback.

21

Once they reached the bottom of the hillside, Pike and Stumpy cut Charley's blood-soaked body down from the tree stump. Luke and the other men, having no shovels, gathered up rocks and respectfully piled them atop the corpse, protecting it from scavengers. They made sure the grave faced east so that every dawn the rising sun would warm Charley's spirit.

Teddy said a brief prayer at the graveside. No one else spoke. They all felt too depressed to say anything. Charley's death was such a senseless waste of a good human being that it defied explanation. Luke was by no means a religious person, nor did he expect people to be perfect, but he did believe there should be some kind of moral justification for taking a decent man's life; and when there wasn't, like now, he was left speechless.

When Teddy was finished praying, she made it abundantly clear to Luke and the men that she was determined to press on, regardless of the odds, and was in no mood to listen to reason. She then started up the slope. But she hadn't taken more than a few steps when the fourth Comanchero who had collapsed near his dead companions suddenly got to his knees and pistol in hand, ordered Teddy to stop.

Startled, she obeyed and turned toward him.

'Get 'em up,' he barked. 'Same goes for the rest of you,' he told Luke, McClory and the men. 'Or I'll put a goddamn hole right through her.'

Grudgingly, the men started to raise their hands.

But not Luke. His right hand moved with blurring speed. His Colt seemed to jump into it and before the Comanchero could pull the trigger, Luke fired. The bullet punched a hole in the Comanchero's forehead, killing him instantly. He remained kneeling there for a moment as if frozen in time . . . then slumped over onto his face.

No one moved. Mouths agape, they stared disbelievingly at Luke.

Then Teddy, equally shocked by how fast Luke had drawn and fired, lowered her hands.

'Th-thanks, L.C.,' she said shakily.

Uncomfortable in the spotlight Luke holstered his Colt and said: 'Sooner we get moving, Miss Teddy, the faster we'll find the Webbers.'

'He's right,' McClory said. 'C'mon, boys. Back to our horses.'

He and the men started up the hillside, leaving Luke and Teddy alone.

She moved close to him, saying softly: 'You know if I hadn't seen you do that, I never would've believed it was possible.'

'No need to make a big fuss over it,' he said shyly. 'I just happened to get the drop on him is all.'

Teddy looked at him, eyes bright with gratitude and fondness, and slowly shook her head. 'You can downplay it all you like, L.C. You still saved my life and if I want to make a big fuss over it, I will.' She cupped her hands about his face and kissed him.

Surprised, Luke barely had time to kiss her back before she pulled away and with a tiny laugh, continued on up the hill.

They rejoined McClory and the men by their horses. Mounting, they rode back to the trail they were on earlier. There, Luke gathered enough dead grass to make one torch and by its flickering light McClory was able to lead them to the exact spot where the Comanches had attacked him earlier.

'Charley was kneeled right there, examining all the tracks,' McClory said, pointing at some hoof prints on the ground. 'He didn't say anything for the longest time. Then he looked up and grinned at me. 'We're breathing down their necks, boss.'

''How do you know that?'

''One of their horses has gone lame.'

"Mean they're riding double?'

"Not yet. But when it gets worse, and it will, they'll have no choice. Then it's only a matter of time before we run them down." McClory paused, troubled by his memory of Charley, then said to Teddy: 'Those were his last words.'

'You mean that's when the Comanches — ?'

McClory nodded grimly.

'Didn't you or Charley have any inkling before that?' Luke asked. 'You just said they were all around you.'

'They were. But they were quieter than ghosts. Hell, not even Charley heard them and he's half Kiowa. I mean, one second we were talking and the next, he had two arrows sticking in his back.'

His words painted an upsetting picture and no one said anything.

Teddy broke the grim silence. 'All right, listen up. We'll just have to find the Webbers without Charley. It won't be easy but if he's right about the lame horse, they can't have gotten very far.'

'My bet is they kept to the trail,'

Luke said. 'That way there'd be less chance of the lame pony stepping into a hole and breaking its leg. 'Cause if that happened, they'd be forced to double up and we'd be a cinch to catch them.'

'Let's not count our chickens,' Teddy cautioned. 'The Webbers know these hills as well as anybody. Should they leave the trail, which I'm sure in time they will, following their tracks across open scrubland is going to be a nightmare.'

'Maybe not,' McClory mused.

Teddy gave him a testy look. 'If you know something I don't, Thad, now would be the time to tell me.'

'It's just a hunch, Miss Teddy. I could be mistaken.'

'Tell me anyway.'

'Well, years ago when the Webbers first came to the valley, Cody was a miner not a rancher.'

'So?'

'He and his wife, Mona, staked a claim in these hills and worked it until she became pregnant with their first child. She wanted to move back to Santa Rosa, but Cody persuaded her to stay on for a few more months. He worked day and night, digging deeper and deeper into the hill, but never found any color.'

'Color?'

'Ore. Gold . . . silver . . . '

'Go on.'

'The baby was born soon after that, and Mona made Cody quit mining and take up ranching.'

'Is there a point to all this?' Teddy demanded.

'The point,' McClory said emphatically, 'is who would think of looking for the Webbers in an abandoned mine shaft?'

'Good question,' Teddy said, now understanding. 'And this mine, Thad? Do you know where it is?'

'I can take you right to it, Miss Teddy.'

'Fair enough. Lead the way.' She signaled to the men to follow McClory. She then wheeled her horse around and rode alongside Luke. 'Keep your eye on Thad,' she said quietly.

'Why? What's wrong?'

'Probably nothing. I'm just surprised that he knew all about this mine is all.'

'Because your father never mentioned it, you mean?'

She shrugged. 'Maybe. I mean Father always tells me everything and . . . well, let's just say I'm a bit uneasy and let it go at that.'

22

True to his word, McClory led them through the now-moonlit hills to the abandoned mine. The entrance was halfway up a rocky slope and almost hidden by bushes. Nearby, stood an old derelict shack and the remains of a sluice, most of the boards of which had been carried off by other miners for their own use.

Dismounting near the entrance, they fanned out and took cover wherever they could find it. There was no trace of the Webbers. Luke, closest to the bushes growing around the entrance, couldn't see any broken twigs indicating that riders had passed through. The ground was no help either. It was covered in loose shale that did not show hoof-prints and dangerously steep in places. He signaled to Teddy that he'd drawn a blank.

Disgruntled, she turned to McClory, ready to chew him out for wasting their time. Before she could, Luke noticed a fragment of blue material snagged on a bush by the entrance and waved for her to keep quiet.

'If the Webbers are here,' he said to McClory, 'where do you figure they hid their horses?'

'In the tunnel,' McClory replied. 'It's level for the first hundred feet or so. They'd have no trouble hiding three — ' He broke off as a faint nickering came from inside the mine, followed by the sound of a horse nervously stirring around.

They all heard it and Teddy gave McClory an appreciative nod.

'Looks like you were right, after all, Thad,' she whispered.

'Yeah, but we still got to flush them out,' he reminded. 'That won't be no picnic. Somebody's likely to get shot.'

'We could smoke them out,' Luke said. 'Shouldn't be that hard — unless there's another shaft or exit somewhere.'

'There ain't,' McClory said.

He spoke with such conviction that Luke, remembering Teddy's uneasiness, couldn't help asking: 'How come you know so much about this mine?'

McClory turned to Teddy as if she'd asked the question. 'Your pa once considered taking over this claim, along with several others in the area, and had me bring a geologist here to see if the mineral rights were worth anything.'

She frowned, surprised. 'When was this?'

'Long time ago, Miss Teddy, when you were still at boarding school.'

Before McClory could say anymore, Luke said: 'If we're going to smoke the Webbers out of there, Miss Teddy, we ought to get started.'

She nodded, 'Go ahead,' and motioned to the men to help him.

'Once the bushes are burning,' Luke told them, 'get back behind cover.'

'Are you expecting them to come charging out?' Teddy said.

'Either that or they'll open fire, hoping we'll scatter, so they can bust out.'

'Well, no matter what they do,' she said grimly, 'just make sure they don't escape. I've got big plans for them.'

McClory said: 'Shouldn't we first try to talk them out?'

'Why?'

'Might save lives, Miss Teddy.'

'I'm not interested in saving their lives, Thad. Besides,' she added, 'Cody and his sons aren't going to give up without a fight. Would you, if you knew you were facing a rope?'

It was the first time she'd mentioned hanging and Luke and the men looked surprised — and uneasy.

'Well?' she said to Luke. 'You going to light those bushes or do I have to?'

'Whoa, hold on, Miss Teddy. You can't hang the Webbers.'

'Who says I can't?'

'The law, for one thing. Whatever punishment they get will be up to a judge and jury to decide. Stringing them up here would be no different than lynching.'

'That's all they deserve!'

'Just for throwing a lamp through your parlor window?'

'They also set fire to our barn,' she reminded.

'Even so, setting fires ain't a hanging offense.'

'Murder is.'

'What're you talking about? Who'd they murder?'

'No one. But that's not because they didn't try. Attempted murder is just as bad as murder. Don't you understand?' she said when Luke looked puzzled. 'My father's a cripple, confined to a wheelchair. If he'd been trapped alone in the parlor, he would've burned to death!'

'But he wasn't and didn't,' Luke said. 'That's a big difference.'

'Doesn't matter. Cody Webber knew my father was helpless and that didn't stop him. He and his boys went ahead and tossed that lamp through the window anyway. And for that, they're going to hang — even if I have to string them up myself! Now,' she said before he could argue, 'light those damn bushes, L.C., and let's get this over with!' She turned and aimed her rifle at the mine entrance.

Luke looked at McClory and the men. They were no happier about hanging the Webbers than he was, but none of them seemed willing to speak up.

'Miss Teddy,' Luke said, forcefully enough to grab her attention, 'if it's your intention to give these boys a necktie party, count me out.'

'You can't be serious?'

'Try me. What's more, I think you'll find I ain't the only one against it.'

He'd hoped that might stop her. Instead, she turned to McClory, saying: 'Set fire to those bushes, Thad. As for the rest of you,' she said to the men, 'when the Webbers come riding out of there, shoot low so you only hit their horses. I want Cody and his sons alive! You got that? Alive!'

McClory didn't move. He wouldn't look at Teddy either.

'Dammit, Thad, I gave you an order! Set those bushes on fire!'

He uneasily toed the dirt. 'Miss Teddy, I . . . I don't reckon this would sit well with your pa. He can be mighty harsh at times, even vengeful, but long as I've known him, he ain't never lynched no one.'

Teddy glared contemptuously at him. 'Father was right,' she said, 'you *have* gone soft!'

McClory reddened, but didn't say anything.

Teddy turned to the men. 'How about the rest of you — you going to turn weak-sister on me too?'

'Miss Teddy,' Pike said reproachfully, 'you got no right to call us that.'

'He's right,' Stumpy agreed. 'Just 'cause we won't go along with lynching the Webbers, don't mean we're weak-sisters.'

'But it *does* mean you're unemployed!' she snapped. 'How about it?' she asked the rest of the men. 'You willing to lose your jobs over this?'

They stirred uneasily, none of them willing to confront her.

'Bunch of no-good weasels, that's what you are,' she said disgustedly. 'No better than rats deserting a ship.'

The men looked resentful. Most of them scowled at her and for a moment Luke thought they might openly rebel. But they didn't, content to grumble among themselves. A few even looked at Luke as if expecting him to speak for them.

'Be reasonable, Miss Teddy,' Luke urged. 'No one's deserting you. Hell, we're willing to risk getting shot for you. We just ain't up to lynching, that's all.'

'In other words, you want me to hand the Webbers over to that milksop of a sheriff, Lou Eldon?'

'Milksop or not, he *is* the law.'

'Law be damned! He only wears that star because Stillman Stadtlander bought it for him — just like he did when Lonnie Forbes was alive.'

'That still don't add up to a lynching,' Luke said.

Teddy glared about her, gray eyes ablaze with anger. 'Someone give me a match,' she barked.

No one moved.

Furious, she walked up to one of the men and held out her hand to him. 'If you ever want to work in this valley again, Colby, you'll give me a damn match!'

Grudgingly, he obeyed.

Without a word, Teddy crawled to the bushes growing in front of the mine entrance and struck the match on a rock. The tiny flame flared in the darkness, momentarily revealing her as she went to light the bushes.

Before she could, a shot rang out inside the mine.

Teddy gasped as the bullet struck her shoulder, knocking her backward.

'Next one of you tries that,' a man's voice warned from in the mine shaft, 'won't live to see sunup.'

'Damn you!' Luke yelled. 'You bastards just signed your death warrant!' He quickly scrambled up the slope to Teddy and grabbed her legs, ready to pull her back. Another pair of hands helped him and he realized

McClory had crawled up beside him. Luke nodded his thanks and together they half-carried, half-dragged Teddy back behind the nearest rock.

'Let 'em have it,' Luke told the men.

They all opened fire. There was a deafening roar as their bullets shredded the bushes and ricocheted off the inner walls of the mine shaft. Inside, someone yelped in pain and began to curse.

'Keep shooting,' Luke yelled as some of the men stopped. 'Don't quit until those sonsofbitches are either dead or come crawling out of there!'

As everyone resumed firing, Luke cradled Teddy in his arms while McClory gently unbuttoned her shirt and pressed his wadded kerchief over the bleeding wound. She flinched, eyes watering, but made no sound. Luke wanted to tell her how much he cared for her but as usual, couldn't find the words. Instead he gently kissed her on the forehead. McClory frowned, surprised by Luke's affection. But he kept his thoughts to himself and forming a sling with one sleeve of her jacket, slipped her arm through it.

'How bad is it?' Luke asked him.

'I've seen worse. Bullet missed the bone and went clean through.'

Barely able to hear him above all the shooting, Luke leaned close to Teddy and spoke in her ear. 'You're going to be fine.'

Eyes slits, teeth gritted against the pain, she nodded to show she understood.

'We got to get her back to the ranch,' Luke told McClory.

He nodded. 'Take a couple of the boys to help you. Rest of us will stay here and keep the Webbers pinned down.'

Teddy started to protest. But Luke pressed his finger over her lips, saying: 'This ain't up for discussion, Miss Teddy. Your pa would have me skinned alive if I didn't bring you home.'

'B-but what about the — Webbers?'

'You leave them to me,' McClory said.

'S-swear you w-won't let them get away?'

141

'Next time you see these jaspers,' he promised, 'they'll be behind bars.' To Luke, he added: 'Once you're clear of the hills, send Pike to get Doc Talbot.'

'Will do.' Luke signaled to Pike and Brock Cooper to help him. They came scrambling over and between them, they carried Teddy to the horses at the base of the slope. Though she was in great pain and couldn't move her right arm, she told them to put her into the saddle, adding that she could ride alone.

Luke and Pike lifted her onto her horse while Brock gently guided her boots into the stirrups. Once she was settled, Luke gave her the reins and mounted his horse. Then with Pike riding on her right side and Brock her left, he took the lead and they slowly rode back through the moon-spackled hills, the roar of gunfire gradually fading behind them.

23

It was almost dawn by the time they reached the valley. Reining up at the foot of the hills, Luke told Pike to ride to Santa Rosa and wake up Doc Talbot. 'Tell him Miss Teddy's been shot and we need him at the ranch.'

'What if he won't come?' Pike said. 'You know doc. Ever since his wife passed, he can be mighty cantankerous at times.'

'If he gives you any trouble,' Luke said grimly, 'stick your iron in his ribs.'

'You mean that?'

Luke nodded. 'Bring him at gunpoint if you have to, but bring the SOB.'

'Okay,' Pike said reluctantly. 'You're the boss.' He rode off.

Luke turned to Teddy. She looked ghostly pale and ready to fall out of the saddle.

Worried, he said: 'You want to rest up

a spell, Miss Teddy, or do you reckon you can make it to the ranch?'

''Course I can make it,' she snapped. 'Now quit fussing, L.C., and for heaven's sake let's get going.'

He bit back a sharp retort and guided his horse alongside her. Then with Brock still riding on her left, the three of them rode in the direction of the ranch.

After a few miles the sun started inching above the hills behind them. It felt warm on Luke's back and its glowing light painted the open scrub-land a pale primrose. It also cast weird, elongated shadows that stretched out before them like distorted images in a broken mirror.

Adding to the eeriness, a distant coyote greeted the dawn with a mournful yip-yipping howl.

As if triggered by the sound, Teddy said suddenly: 'I was wrong.'

''Bout what?' Luke asked.

'Thad. Accusing him of hiding something.'

'You didn't accuse him, Miss Teddy. You just said you felt uneasy about him knowing so much about the mine.'

'I was still wrong.'

'Maybe so. But knowing you, something must've triggered it.'

'If it did, I've no idea what it was.'

'How about your pa?'

'What about him?'

'Did he say something about McClory — something to discredit him?'

'No,' she said. Then, as it hit her: 'Yes.'

'What was it?'

'Said that Thad had gone soft. You were there, remember?'

Luke didn't but nodded anyway.

'I guess I took it to heart and . . . ' Teddy paused and sighed regretfully. 'My God, I wish I could take it back.'

'You can always apologize later.'

If she heard him, she didn't show it. They rode on in silence. Presently, far-off, the coyote gave another mournful howl. Again, the noise triggered a response from Teddy. As if reminding herself, she said: 'Thad's a square-shooter, if there ever was one.'

'Sure seems like,' Luke agreed.

'I don't know how I could ever have let myself become suspicious of him. He's never given me any reason to question his loyalty or his advice. But for some reason, when it came to the Webbers and that mine, I just . . . ' She broke off, frowning, as if questioning herself, then said: 'It's so unlike me. You can ask anyone, they'll tell you. I'm for law and order all the way. Yet, for a while back there, I surely wanted to lynch the Webbers.'

'Anger can do strange things to a person,' Luke said. 'So can fear.'

'Fear?'

'You were afraid for your pa's life, remember?'

She gave a dismissive shrug. 'That's still no excuse to turn on a man who's been loyal to my father since the start. Good heavens, without Thad's help, Father never could've built Shadow Hills into the ranch it is today. And he'd be the first to admit it. No,' she continued after a pause, 'let's face it. This wasn't really about Thad or my questioning his loyalty.'

'What, then?'

'It was about me. Me and my never-ending desire to please Father . . . to make him proud of me.'

'From what I've seen, Miss Teddy, you've already done that and more.'

'Well, never again,' she said as if he hadn't spoken. 'I'm done trying to be someone other than myself. And I'm done trying to please him. From now on, to hell with it! If Father doesn't like the way I'm running things, let him replace me.'

'He'd never do that.'

'I'm willing to step aside any time he says. If he wants someone else at the reins, let him hire someone. Or better still, turn them over to you.'

'Me?' Luke laughed cynically. 'Thanks, but no thanks. I've no interest in being responsible for anything. And that includes being in charge.'

Teddy didn't say anything. He looked at her and saw she was staring straight ahead as if lost in her thoughts. He knew then she hadn't heard a word he'd said.

'Father likes you,' she said abruptly. 'Says he trusts you and values your opinion. Well, so be it. With my shoulder like it is, I'm going to be out of action for a while anyway. So the timing's perfect.'

Luke started to say that the timing was anything but perfect. But what was the point? Like her father, he knew that once Teddy made up her mind about something, nothing on God's earth could ever change it.

So he kept his opinion to himself and with the rising sun warming their backs, they rode on in silence, their ever-changing shadows dancing ahead of them.

24

When they finally arrived at the ranch dawn had broken and pink clouds drifted lazily overhead. Reining up in front of the house, Luke dismounted and helped Teddy down from her horse. Though she didn't complain he knew by her gritted teeth and dazed expression that pain was making her dizzy. Telling Brock to handle the horses, Luke grasped her arm and helped her to the porch.

As they climbed the steps, the front door opened and Dr. Fulton Talbot came out. Luke had only met him once before when the doctor came to the ranch to tend to Luther Austin, but he'd heard numerous rumors about him. A tall, slim, dark-haired widower in his mid-forties, Talbot had once been one of the most-beloved men in Santa Rosa. But a few years back he'd lost his wife to cancer and her death turned his world upside down. Unable to face life without her, he'd started hitting the bottle. The townspeople, understanding his grief, at first gave him a pass. But eventually his heavy drinking drove them away, ruining his practice. Then, from what Luke had heard, a few months ago Dr. Talbot had waked from a drunken binge to find himself in church. He couldn't remember how he got there, but believing it to be a sign from God he'd turned to religion and abruptly — miraculously, some folks said — stopped drinking and built up his practice again.

Now, as the doctor approached Teddy, he looked sleepy but cold sober.

'Well, young lady,' he gently chided, 'I reckon you've got yourself in a fine mess.'

Teddy gave a weak smile but didn't have the strength to answer.

'She's lucky, doc,' Luke said. 'The bullet went right through.'

'There's nothing lucky about being

shot,' Dr. Talbot said, adding: 'Now, if you'll be so kind, young fella, please bring Miss Teddy inside.' He opened the door for them, and Luke gently guided Teddy into the house. Once inside, Dr. Talbot took her other arm and together they helped her along the hallway and into the parlor. Here, her father sat alone in his wheelchair, wrapped in a bathrobe, his sunken unshaven face creased with concern.

Dr. Talbot helped Luke sit Teddy in one of the chairs at the table. Then he opened his black bag and asked the two men to leave.

'I'm not going anywhere till I know how my daughter is,' Austin said firmly.

'Father, please . . . ' Teddy begged. 'Do as Dr. Talbot says.'

'I'm sure she'll be okay, sir,' Luke added.

For a moment Austin seemed about to refuse. Then he grudgingly nodded and motioned for Luke to wheel him to the door. There, he looked back at his daughter with affection and said fondly:

'Don't worry, little girl, I'll be right outside.'

She managed a weak smile and mouthed 'thank you' to him.

Luke wheeled him out into the hall, where Rivera was waiting. The proud *pistolero* looked disheveled, as if he'd dressed hurriedly and came over as soon as he saw them.

Ignoring him, Austin gave Luke a grateful smile. 'I owe you, L.C.'

'For what, sir?'

'Bringing my daughter home safely.'

'Just keeping my promise, Mr. Austin.'

'Promises are cheap, son. Keeping them — now that's a rarity.'

Luke didn't know what to say so he gave a noncommittal shrug.

'One last thing,' Austin said. 'What happened to the Webbers?'

'When I rode off,' Luke replied, 'McClory and the boys had all three of them trapped in an old mine.'

'How long ago was that?'

'Before sunup. By now, hopefully he's smoked them out and taken them to

Santa Rosa to hand them over to the sheriff.'

'Sheriff?' Austin exclaimed disgustedly. 'Lou Eldon, now there's a pathetic excuse for a lawman if there ever was one. I swear he's worse than Lonnie Forbes ever was. Well, no matter. I want you to go find Thad, wherever he is, and tell him to bring the Webbers here, to me.'

'But — '

'Just do it, son. That's an order.' Before Luke could argue, Austin motioned to Rivera and the tall thin *pistolero* wheeled him away.

25

Luke was worn out from riding and the last thing he wanted to do was get back in the saddle and try to find McClory. But he also wanted to keep his job and knew if he defied the old man he'd be fired. So taking pity on his exhausted horse, he turned it loose in the corral and saddled the big gray mustang he'd recently broken.

Some stallions had long memories. They remembered the wrangler who broke them and tried to bite or kick him whenever he was close. But the high-spirited gray didn't seem to bear Luke any ill will. Grateful, Luke stepped up into the saddle. He'd already decided to wait for McClory and the men in Santa Rosa, hoping by now they had captured the Webbers, and was in no mood to be hassled by an unruly horse.

The gray had a long powerful stride

that was smooth and easy on the spine, and occasionally during the ride Luke found himself dozing in the warm sunshine.

The miles passed quickly and they reached Blanco Canyon sooner than Luke had expected. He slowed the stallion to a loping gait and followed the ancient dry riverbed that served as a trail, snaking between the steep, dazzling white limestone cliffs. The sunlight bouncing off them was hard on the eyes and Luke pulled the brim of his old flat-crowned Stetson lower so he could see without squinting. The riverbed was rock-hard and pitted with shallow cracks and holes. A lesser horse, unfamiliar with the terrain, might have stumbled and lost its footing. But the former mustang had roamed this country since its birth and nimbly avoided all the pitfalls, carrying Luke through the canyon without a single mishap.

Now all that was between him and Santa Rosa was a range of low brown hills and a wide stretch of open scrubland.

He lightly tapped the gray with his spurs and it cheerfully responded, its loping stride effortlessly carrying Luke up a hill that crested at a rocky outcrop. He reined up once he reached the rocks to give the gray a breather. Below him, the land sloped down to the cattle pens beside the railroad station at the edge of town. Thanks to the affections of a pretty and obliging maid who'd once worked at the Carlisle Hotel, Luke was no stranger to Santa Rosa and after a little he nudged the gray on down the hill toward the tracks.

Entering town he picked up Front, a broad dirt street that had once been a wagon trail but was now the main thoroughfare. Traffic was heavy. He slowed the gray stallion to a walk and joined the riders and freight wagons moving in both directions between the stores, saloons and offices lining each side of the street.

The sheriff's office and jail was in a low, wood-and-adobe building in the center of town. Luke passed Gustafson's Livery, MacKenzie's Mercantile, Harley's

Food-and-Grain store and the Carlisle Hotel before reaching the office. As he reined in, he noticed McClory's long-legged piebald tied up in front of the Steer Horn Saloon opposite. Taking that to mean the Webbers were now locked up, Luke dismounted, tied up the sweaty, tireless gray and entered the office.

Sheriff Lou Eldon was in his favorite position: leaned back in his chair, long legs propped up on the desk, gnarly hands clasped across his belly, dozing in the heat. He was a huge man, with dark graying hair and a florid face, who topped Luke by several inches.

Luke cleared his throat. When that didn't wake the lawman, Luke kicked the desk, startling him awake. The sheriff blinked owlishly at him. Then recognizing Luke, he brought his legs down, sat up and wiped the back of his hand across his dry, cracked lips.

'Well, well, so you finally made it,' he growled. 'McClory said you'd be here. What took you so long?'

Not wanting to get caught up in one

of the sheriff's boring, long-winded conversations, Luke ignored his question and said: 'The Webbers, did McClory bring them in in one piece?'

'Pretty much. While he and the men were smoking them out of a cave or somewhere, Cody got nicked in the shoulder. But the doc patched him up and his sons are okay. McClory's across the street, you know.'

'Yeah, I saw his horse.' Luke paused, wondering how to say what was on his mind, then decided to plow right in. 'Did he say anything about Mr. Austin?'

'Only that he — McClory, I mean — sent the men back to the ranch to tell the Old Man that the Webbers were under lock and key. Why? Should I be expecting trouble?'

'Could be. Mr. Austin's dead set on seeing the Webbers hang.'

'Whoa, hold on,' Sheriff Eldon said. 'Did I miss something? I thought this little fracas was about the Webbers setting fire to Mr. Austin's barn and house.'

'It was — is.'

'Well, that'll buy them some jail time but it ain't a hanging offense.'

'Tell that to Mr. Austin. I did and got nowhere fast.'

The sheriff sighed, and taking the makings out of his shirt pocket began rolling a smoke. 'Dammit, I should've known this wasn't going to end up being a simple matter of arson! I mean, anything involving that crippled old bastard always gets blown out of proportion.' He licked the cigarette paper, pinched it together with thumb and forefinger and put the smoke between his lips. 'Got a light?'

Luke dug out a match, flared it on the desk and held the flame under the lawman's cigarette.

'Thanks,' he said, spitting out a stream of smoke. 'So tell me, what're the chances of Luther Austin and his boys riding in here to string up the Webbers?'

'It's possible.'

'Aw, hell, L.C., don't sugarcoat it. Tell me the truth. The Webbers' lives may depend on it.'

'He'll be here. With his men. Guns blazing. You can take that to the bank.'

Sheriff Eldon considered Luke's answer, inhaled and slowly expelled the smoke in a loud, drawn-out sigh. 'I won't be able to stop him. You know that, don't you?'

'Then maybe you should sneak the Webbers out of town.'

'In broad daylight?'

'I'll help you. So will McClory. We could take them out the back way and — ' Luke stopped as the door swung open and in hurried a young, carrot-haired cowboy he'd never seen before.

'I'm Will Mason,' he said. 'This fella, McClory, who's in the Steer Horn across the street told me to tell you what I saw.'

'We're listening,' Sheriff Eldon said.

'Little while ago as I was coming in town, I saw all these riders crossing the flats. There must've been thirty or more of them, all headed this way.'

160

'Was Luther Austin with them?' Luke asked.

'Yeah. Riding in a wagon driven by that old Mex' who works for him.'

'Manuel Rivera?'

'Yeah, that's him.'

'So you were right after all,' Sheriff Eldon said to Luke. Then to the young cowboy: 'Thanks for the tip, *amigo*.'

'Anytime.' The young cowboy hurried out.

Luke looked at the sheriff. 'Your call, Eldon.'

'Thanks for nothing.' Rising, he ground out his smoke and put on his hat.

'Where you going?'

'Well,' he drawled, 'I don't know about you, L.C., but this is one fight I don't aim to get mixed up in.'

'There's still time to sneak the Webbers out of town.'

'Then *you* sneak 'em out. Me, I'll be too busy riding over to Stadtlander's place. I was supposed to meet him there tomorrow morning, but, guess what, the meeting's just been changed to today.'

'For chrissake, sheriff, you can't run out now!'

'No? Watch me.' He took the cell keys off a hook on the wall and tossed them to Luke. 'They're all yours, *amigo.*'

''Mean you're willing to let the Webbers be lynched?'

Sheriff Eldon chuckled sourly. 'Not in front of me, no.'

'So you're turning tail?'

'Damn right!' He started for the door then stopped and looked back at Luke. 'See, that's the difference between you and me, L.C. I *know* who I am. What's more, I know my limitations.'

'And being yellow doesn't bother you?'

'Most of the time, no. And on rare occasions, when it does, I remind myself that a man like me can't suddenly grow a set overnight. I am what I am: a sheriff whose star was paid for by a greedy, ruthless sonofabitch named Stadtlander.'

'And you can live with that?'

'Like Lonnie Forbes always used to say: Man's got to eat. Besides, I like it here. Santa Rosa's the perfect fit for me. Quiet, full of hard-working folks, and far enough off the beaten track so that none of the great cattle drives from Texas ever come through it. That means I never have to deal with any wild, rip-snorting, let's-get-drunk-and-shoot-up-the-town drovers that most lawmen face each year. Oh, sure, I'm no Wyatt Earp or Bill Hickok and never pretended to be. But I'm good enough to keep the peace here and these days, what more can the average citizen ask for?'

'I hate to think.'

'Then don't. Thinking can get you killed, L.C. And so will hanging around here trying to protect the Webbers from a rope. What's more, they ain't worth it. I mean, ask yourself — would they do the same for you? Hell, no! What sane man would? Be smart for once, *amigo*. Walk away while you still can.' He started out, but before the door closed, stuck his head back in, adding: 'Keys for the shotguns in the rack are in my top drawer. Help yourself.' His head disappeared and the door slammed shut behind him.

Now why can't you do like he says, Luke wondered, and be smart for once?

It was one of those questions that a man should never ask himself, because the truth is when it came to possibly dying for someone else or a cause there was no common sense answer. Every now and then a man finds himself confronted by an unanswerable question, often through no fault of his own, as if life was testing his moral fiber in order to see what kind of mettle he was made of.

This, Luke realized all too clearly, was one of those times. And not wanting to lose his nerve, he quickly pushed any thought of leaving out of his mind and cursed himself for whining about the hand he'd been dealt.

26

Shotgun over one arm, Luke stood in the shade outside the sheriff's office constantly looking from one end of Front Street to the other, all the time wondering how long it would be before he got his first glimpse of Austin and his men.

He'd never felt more alone in his life, which was why he was glad when he saw Thad McClory emerge from the Steer Horn and cross the street toward him. The foreman carried a double-barreled sawed-off and his pockets bulged with shells.

'I see you heard?' he said as he joined Luke on the boardwalk.

'You know what they say about bad news.'

'All too well, unfortunately. Where are the Webbers?'

'Still behind bars.'

'And the sheriff?'

'Riding like hell for Stadtlander's ranch.'

McClory grinned ruefully. 'Some folks never change, do they?'

'If we were smart,' Luke said, 'we'd be riding with him.'

'It's a thought that's crossed my mind more than once. Don't think it ain't.'

'Yet you're still here?'

'So are you.'

'Shows how smart we are.'

'Fear's nothing to be afraid of. Not if you got it under control.'

'I'd settle for that, if I only knew how.'

'Just takes the right amount of determination.'

'Determination, uh?'

'Without it, you're licked before you start. I mean, think about it, *compadre*. What sane person wants to face danger or worse, death, when every instinct and grain of common sense is telling him to jump on his pony and ride?'

'Only us apparently,' Luke said, adding: 'What about the Webbers?'

'What about them?'

'Do you reckon we should arm them, just in case we can't persuade Austin and his boys to back off?'

'That thought occurred to me too. But the problem then is we'll be showing the old man our hand before we have to. He could then decide to turn this into an all-out gunfight and to be honest, that's the last goddamn thing I want.'

Before Luke could agree with him, he heard something and held up his hand for silence. 'Hear that?'

'Riders, yeah,' McClory said grimly. 'Reckon doomsday's on its way.'

The two of them stood there in stony silence, listening to the approaching hoof-beats. The sound slowly loudened, like approaching thunder, hiding the thud-thudding of their hearts.

The riders were close now.

'Here they come,' McClory said, thumbing toward the west end of town.

Luke looked and saw a cloud of swirling dust coming along Front Street. For a few moments that's all either of them could see. Then the lead riders rode out of the dust into the sunlight like avenging ghosts.

They were in no hurry. They held their horses at a slow deliberate walk, each man grimly resolute and dangerous.

They were escorting a small wagon driven — as the young cowboy said — by the old Mexican *pistolero*. Sitting beside Rivera was Luther Austin. The embittered rancher wore a pale gray, high-crowned Stetson pulled low over his eyes and had a blanket draped about his frail, hunched-over shoulders. Something glinted on his lap. And as they came closer, Luke saw it was a side-by-side shotgun, the same beautiful 12-gauge he'd seen resting on pegs above the parlor fireplace.

'Love him or hate him,' McClory said grudgingly, 'you can't help but admire the old bastard. He never shirks a fight.

Comes straight at you.'

'Yeah,' Luke said, 'and hell's coming with him.'

27

As Luke stood beside McClory, staring out into the bright sunlight at Luther Austin, he wondered if he really could shoot him if he had to. And if he did, how it would affect his relationship with Teddy? Could she still love a man, any man, who shot her father?

It was another of those unanswerable questions.

The war party was close now. There were so many riders they filled the street. Through the dust kicked up by their horses Luke could see folks on the opposite boardwalk stopping to gawk. He knew they were waiting to see if McClory and he got killed and he had a sudden urge to chase them away with a load of buckshot. Luckily, sanity ruled. He took his fingers off the triggers and turned back to the advancing riders. They were a scary sight. Even though he knew most of them, he also knew if it came to a shootout whose side they would take and how it would turn out; namely, with Thad and him lying face-down in the dirt.

It was an ugly thought. But wise or foolish it was the choice he'd made and now he had to find the guts to face it.

He grimly watched as Austin and his men slowly reined up in front of him. For several moments no one spoke. All Luke could hear was the horses chewing on their bits, riders stirring in their saddles, their stirrups squeaking. Then as the dust settled, Luke knew it was up to him to set the table and as firmly and convincingly as he could, said:

'This is all wrong, Mr. Austin.'

'Right or wrong,' the old man said harshly, 'it's none of your business.'

'I'm making it my business, sir.'

'So am I,' added McClory.

'That's a mistake that could cost you both your lives.'

'Ours — *and* a lot of others,' Luke

171

said, leveling the shotgun. 'Now, tell your men to turn around.'

'Not a chance in hell.'

Luke didn't say anything but felt his fingers tightening against the triggers.

'I'm warning you for the last time,' Austin hissed. 'Get out of my way!'

'You're wasting your breath, sir.'

Austin, his frail body sagging, said: 'Son, I think you know I like you and I owe you for saving Teddy's life. But the Webbers tried to kill me and I'm going to hang them for it, and if you or anyone else gets in my way, my men will gun you down like rabid dogs in the street.'

'You'll never live to see it,' McClory said.

'And neither will some of you,' Luke told the men.

They stirred uneasily, their grim expressions revealing how much they didn't want to be there.

Austin, sensing he was losing their loyalty, glared at Luke. 'Go ahead, pull the goddamn trigger. It won't change anything.' To his men, he added: 'Soon as he shoots me, gun both of these sonofabitches down. Clear?'

Again, the men shifted uneasily in their saddles.

'Boys,' Luke warned, 'don't let one bitter old man make murderers out of you. And if you kill me or Thad, here, just to please him, that's what you'll be.'

'Think carefully about that,' McClory cautioned. 'Do you really want our deaths on your conscience and a posse on your tail?'

'Besides,' Luke added, 'it ain't like the Webbers are getting off free. They won't hang, and they shouldn't, but they'll definitely serve time for what they've done. Surely, that's justice enough?'

His words hit home. The men swapped looks, all nodding in agreement.

'Be reasonable, will you?' Luke begged Austin. 'Let a judge decide the fate of the Webbers. With me and your daughter as witnesses, they — '

Too late Luke realized he'd pushed

the old man too far. Overcome with anger, Austin shouted, 'Damn you!' and grabbing the side-by-side, raised it to shoot Luke.

Knowing he would kill Rivera as well as Austin if he used the scattergun, Luke jerked his Colt and snapped off a shot. The bullet knocked the shotgun from Austin's claw-like hands, and it fell to the footboard.

'For God's sake,' Luke said as the old man reached for it, 'don't make me kill you!'

He was talking to a deaf man. Enraged, Austin picked up the 12-gauge.

As Luke started to shoot him, a voice cried out: 'Father, no! Don't!'

Austin froze.

So did Luke.

All the men whirled around. Then seeing who it was, they backed up their horses to let a buckboard pass through.

Driving it was Teddy.

Luke barely recognized her. Her long red-gold hair was a tangled mess, her clothes covered in trail dust, and she was pale and exhausted from her wild drive. Racked with pain and sustaining herself by guts alone, she sat slumped over on the seat, a bloodstain reddening her shirt above the sling holding her right arm.

Stopping the buckboard between them, she shook her head in disgust.

'Men,' she exclaimed angrily. 'How much mindless killing will it take before you come to your senses?'

No one said a word.

'As for you,' she told her father, 'I can't believe I used to look up to you. My God, what the hell was I thinking?'

'Teddy, please,' he begged. 'Go home!'

'I'd love to,' she said bitterly. 'But thanks to you, I no longer have a home.'

Her remark crushed him. He gave an anguished sob, as if all the life had been squeezed out of him, and lowered his head so no one would see his grief.

Teddy turned to Luke. 'If you still want me, L.C., I'm ready to go with you right now, any place you say just so long as it's nowhere near here!'

That was good enough for Luke. Holstering his Colt, he handed his shotgun to McClory and stepped off the boardwalk.

'On one condition,' he told Teddy as he reached the buckboard.

'Name it,' she said.

'You and your pa sort this out first.'

'Are you *loco*?'

'Not *that* loco.'

She frowned at him, confused. 'But I thought you said — '

Luke cut her off. 'Listen, Teddy, what I'm trying to say is if you leave now, without patching things up, you'll regret it for the rest of your days.'

'H-How do you know?'

'From personal experience, unfortunately.'

'B-But . . . what if I don't want to patch things up?'

'Do it anyway. Not for now. For the future.'

'What future?'

'Our future. Together.' When she didn't

say anything, he said: 'Our feelings for each other won't last if you always hate your pa. That hate will eat away at you, at us, until you're so consumed with it you won't have any room for love, or me, or anyone else for that matter.'

She frowned angrily, and for a moment he thought he'd lost her.

'Please, Teddy, trust me. I know all about these feelings.'

'How — because of the way you felt about *your* father?'

'Not my father.'

'Who, then?'

'Someone I once loved like a father, a man named Judd Ames who loved me too and treated me like his son . . . ' Luke hesitated, reluctant to drag up memories that still hurt so bad he'd blocked them out since childhood. Then knowing if he wanted to keep Teddy, he had no choice, he said: 'Trouble was, I loved that old man so much my thinking got all twisted. I became so afraid Judd might leave me one day, I ran off first, before he could.

It took me a while to come to my senses and go back to the ranch, and by then it was too late. Judd was dead.'

'Oh my God,' Teddy exclaimed. 'How? What happened?'

''Cording to the men, Judd blamed himself for driving me off. It chewed and chewed on him until one night he got all liquored up . . . wandered off into a storm and drowned in a flash flood.'

'Oh, L.C., how awful. I'm so sorry.'

Luke shrugged off her sympathy. 'This ain't about me, Miss Teddy. It's about you and your pa. You're both stubborn, like I was, and if you walk away now, while you're angry, it'll only grow worse . . . until it gets so out-of-proportion, you won't never be able to fix it.'

Teddy didn't say anything. She turned to her father. He was now looking at her, his expression asking for forgiveness, and though Teddy still seemed angry Luke sensed her resolve was weakening.

'Dammit, you two, will you listen to Luke?' a voice barked behind them.

Everyone turned toward the Carlisle Hotel, where Delores Austin stood outside the entrance.

'What're you doing here?' Teddy said angrily.

'She's taking the afternoon train to Las Cruces,' her father said.

Teddy frowned, confused. 'Train?'

'Yeah. She decided to leave me.'

The news surprised everyone; especially Luke and Teddy.

Delores smiled ruefully at her husband. 'Thanks for being a gentleman, Luther dear. But your daughter deserves the truth.' To Teddy, she added: 'Your father finally grew tired of my infidelity and showed me the door.'

Teddy, even more surprised, said: 'And you didn't try to talk him out of it?'

'It crossed my mind,' Delores admitted. 'But then I realized it was the best thing for both of us. Your father deserves a wife who loves only him' — she smiled sadly at Austin for a moment before turning back to Teddy — 'and I deserve to live in the city where I can enjoy the finer things in life . . . not to mention the company of men who don't stink of cattle and only talk about whorehouses and trail drives.' Pausing, she scanned all the horsemen gathered before her, 'With one exception,' and then let her gaze settle on Luke. 'And unfortunately, he wasn't interested in me.' She sighed regretfully, turned and went back into the hotel.

28

Teddy looked at her father, saw his tears of hopeful expectancy and melted. Stretching out her arms to Luke, she said: 'Help me down, L.C, will you, please?'

He couldn't obey her fast enough. And once Teddy was in his arms, he carried her to the wagon. Rivera quickly jumped down, making room for her, and Luke gently lifted her onto the seat beside her father.

They hugged each other, bringing smiles to everyone's faces.

Luke rejoined McClory on the boardwalk. The foreman gave him back the shotgun and looked happily at Teddy and her father.

'I've waited a long time to see them two make up. Now, thanks to you, kid, I got my wish.'

'Don't call me kid,' Luke said. But he

was smiling as he said it.

McClory grinned and draped his arm fondly around Luke's shoulders. 'I reckon this calls for a drink.'

'Only if you're buying, boss.'

'I wouldn't have it any other way,' McClory said, adding: 'C'mon, let's go bend an arm or two. We got some things to discuss.'

'Like, what?'

'When you was a young'un.'

Luke stopped abruptly and frowned at the foreman.

''Mean when I was at the orphanage?'

'Uh-uh. Before that. When you and your ma was still a family.'

'Me and Ma?' Luke looked confused. 'Why the hell do you want to talk about that?'

'No, no,' McClory said, dragging him toward the saloon. 'First, whiskey — *then* talk.'

'Okay,' Luke said. 'But what you're asking may take more than one drink.'

'We got plenty of time,' McClory

replied. 'Rest of our lives in fact. Now, keep walking, son.'

Luke shrugged and without another word the two of them crossed the street. They walked shoulder-to-shoulder, shotguns held down at their sides, all the riders backing up their horses so the two men could make their way to the Steer Horn for a much-needed drink.

With Ben Bridges:
THREE RIDE AGAIN
SHADOW HORSE
THE OKLAHOMBRES

We do hope that you have enjoyed reading this large print book.

Did you know that all of our titles are available for purchase?

We publish a wide range of high quality large print books including:
Romances, Mysteries, Classics
General Fiction
Non Fiction and Westerns

Special interest titles available in large print are:
The Little Oxford Dictionary
Music Book, Song Book
Hymn Book, Service Book

Also available from us courtesy of Oxford University Press:
Young Readers' Dictionary
(large print edition)
Young Readers' Thesaurus
(large print edition)

For further information or a free brochure, please contact us at:
Ulverscroft Large Print Books Ltd.,
The Green, Bradgate Road, Anstey,
Leicester, LE7 7FU, England.
Tel: (00 44) **0116 236 4325**
Fax: (00 44) **0116 234 0205**

Other titles in the
Linford Western Library:

BLIZZARD JUSTICE

Randolph Vincent

After frostbite crippled the fingers of his gun hand, Isaac Morgan thought his days of chasing desperadoes were over. But when steel-hearted Deputy US Marshal Ambrose Bishop rides into town one winter evening, aiming to bait a trap for a brutal gang which has been terrorizing the border, Morgan's peace is shattered. For after the lawman's scheme misfires, and the miscreants snatch the town judge's beautiful daughter Kitty, Bishop and Morgan must join forces to get her back.

DYNAMITE EXPRESS

Gillian F. Taylor

Sheriff Alec Lawson has come a long way from the Scottish Highlands to Colorado. Life here is never slow as he deals with a kidnapped Chinese woman, moonshine that's turning its consumers blind, and a terrifying incident with an uncoupled locomotive which sees him clinging to the roof of a speeding train car. When a man is found dead out in the wild, Lawson wonders if the witness is telling him the whole truth, and decides to dig a little deeper . . .

HANGING DAY

Rob Hill

Facing the noose after being wrong-
fully convicted of his wife's murder,
Josh Tillman breaks out of jail. Rather
than go on the run, he heads home,
determined to prove his innocence
and track down the real killer. But
he has no evidence or witnesses to
back up his story; his father-in-law
wants him dead; a corrupt prison
guard is pursuing him; and the preacher
who speaks out in his defence is held
at gunpoint for his trouble . . .

APACHE SPRING

J. D. Kincaid

When a stagecoach bound for El Paso is held up by bandits, all but one of the passengers are massacred. Young Lizzie Reardon, a teacher about to take up a post in the school at Burro Creek, is the sole survivor — but, as she has seen the attackers' faces, she is now their target. Deputy Sheriff Frank McCoy joins forces with the famous Kentuckian gunfighter Jack Stone to defend her — but will they succeed?

LYNCHING AT PROSPECT FALLS

Jack Matthews

Town marshal Matt Walker becomes increasingly worried when his young nephew Joey Crane disappears on his way to visit his uncle. All clues point in the direction of Prospect Falls, a town owned and controlled by wealthy rancher H.J. Copeland of the Bar C — whose cattle are rustled on a regular basis. But the thieving gang is actually led by his own foreman, and anyone caught straying onto ranch land is lynched to divert attention from the real culprits . . .

THE MAGNIFICENT MENDOZAS

Ross Morton

When the Mexican circus ships out of the gringo town of Conejos Blancos, Hart and his ruthless desperadoes are quick off the mark to take over the settlement and the adjacent silver mine. With the sheriff slaughtered and many of the citizens held hostage, two local boys escape, and recruit seven Mexican circus performers to help penetrate the cordon of sentries and free the townspeople. For only the Magnificent Mendozas stand a chance against the Hart gang . . .